The day I broke your heart

The day I broke your heart

PIYUSH GUPTA

Srishti
PUBLISHERS & DISTRIBUTORS

Srishti Publishers & Distributors
A unit of AJR Publishing LLP
212A, Peacock Lane
Shahpur Jat, New Delhi – 110 049
editorial@srishtipublishers.com

First published by
Srishti Publishers & Distributors in 2021

10 9 8 7 6 5 4 3 2 1

This is a work of fiction. Names, characters, places and incidents are either products of the author's imagination or are used fictitiously. Any resemblance to actual events or locales or persons, living or dead, is entirely coincidental. The Banaras Hindu College elections or Uttar Pradesh's Rajya Sabha elections have been used as fictitious events to support the narrative.

Printed and bound in India

Dedicated to the spirit of every lover,
And to every soul departed due to Covid-19,
Hope we move towards a better world.

'If not in this one,
you'll find me in the next life…'

You may have retired, but you'll always be
in my heart. Forever...

MSD (Captain Cool)
Tu mera aj bhi hero.

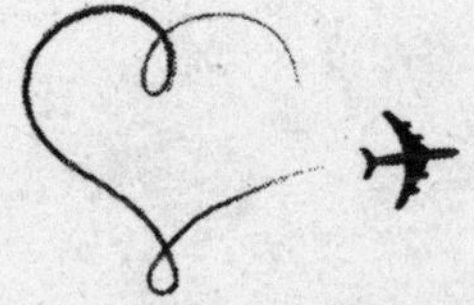

Acknowledgements

If there is something I can do, I can write. If given a chance, I can write all my life.

I take this opportunity to thank my parents, family and friends for providing me with every sort of help I ever needed. Especially my elder sister, Sudha Gupta, who made me believe in this powerful statement, 'One should always follow their heart'.

My brother-in-law, Vishal Gourav, who guided me and was always there to help and support me. Kishan Govinda and Sumit Kr. Gupta, for boosting my enthusiasm.

Ravi Kumar, Deepak Gupta, Ujjwal Gupta and Nirmal Shah, who supported me throughout this journey. I thank you for making this possible and for giving me what I needed at various stages of this journey.

Ashay Chandra, the first reader. Nishant Patel, Sameer Sinha and Faishal Enam, who always stood by my side. Thank you for encouraging me and making me believe what I have written will be loved and accepted worldwide.

I thank everyone who has read my work through this publishing journey; your encouragement made me believe in myself. And then, finally, I became a novelist!

No Going Back

'Are you sure you want to do this?' she asked me as soon as our car stopped.

I took a deep breath and said, 'Thank you for dropping me.' We were quiet, and I was expecting her to say something. I knew what I was doing was right.

For the first time in my life, I was listening to my heart. People would certainly snigger at me if I told them what I was going to do. It was not the most sensible thing. *But has love ever paid heed to logic? It follows its own rhythm.*

I slowly unfastened the seatbelt. She kept holding my hand. I turned to look at her, only to see her beautiful face and teary eyes hiding her insurmountable grief. She tightened her grip on my hand, not wanting me to leave. But, I had no choice.

I slowly released my hand and thought of walking out.

'Dravya, are you sure about this? Think once again,' she said.

'Yes,' I said without hesitation.

A security personnel's knock on the window startled us. 'Please clear the way,' he said.

'I think I should leave,' I told her.

'Dravya, this is the last flight that is taking off.' Her tears rolled down.

'I have to do this for myself,' I said, with unwavering courage infused in me.

'And, what about me?' she asked.

No amount of explanations could justify this to her. I could only imagine what she was going through.

The spread of coronavirus had disrupted our regular lives and shattered our pride. Animals were free and we were caged. China, Italy, Spain and many other countries were under lockdown. India was soon going to be in the same position. Every single day, thousands of people were dying globally. Humanity was in danger.

A fourteen-hour voluntary public curfew was planned on 22 March 2020. From the next day onwards, India was going under complete lockdown for twenty-one days, about which only a privileged few people knew. I was one of them. And I couldn't share this with Khushi.

'I have to go,' I said.

'Why are you doing this?' she asked anxiously.

'I told you, I'm doing this for myself,' I reiterated my reason, which didn't make sense to her.

It wasn't easy. I had no idea what the consequences of this would be. I didn't even know whether what I was going to do was right or wrong? The one thing I was sure about was, I couldn't miss this flight.

'You still love her…?' Khushi said hesitantly.

'Yes,' I said, not being able to look at her.

'I wish you loved me that much,' she said, teary-eyed.

'Khushi,' I moved closer to wipe her tears.

I pulled her mask down and saw her smiling. She didn't want me to go, I could understand her.

'What can I do to make it easier for you?' I asked, not knowing what to do.

'Don't catch this flight,' she responded.

'You know I can't do that,' I said.

'Then come back safely,' she said smiling.

'Hmm... I'll do that. Can I go now?' I asked again.

'Who am I to decide that?' she asked, with a tone of sadness.

'Khushi... Why are you making this tough for me?' I asked helplessly.

'Leaving me was never tough for you,' she said.

'Why would you say that?' I asked.

'Because that is the truth,' she replied.

The pandemic had turned the world upside down and now it was time for India to buckle up. People were nervous, scared and stumped. For the first time in the history of the nation, India was going under complete lockdown.

Even though the Indian economy was going to collapse, a nationwide lockdown seemed to be the only solution. I could sense what was going to happen in a couple of days.

'What's Sid's opinion?' Khushi asked after a moment. Her voice brought me back from the fears and apprehensions which were invading my mind.

'He said I'm crazy. He even said that I'm making the biggest mistake of my life,' I told her honestly.

'Rightly so!' Khushi added.

'Maybe...' I murmured.

'Dravya, at least listen to your best friend. We all can't be wrong.'

'Even I'm not wrong,' I added.

'You are!' Khushi said, a little louder this time. 'Look, I'm sorry,' she apologized soon after. 'I don't want to end this with a row. I don't want to lose you,' she said softly. 'At any cost! You mean a lot to me. You're my life. Why don't you understand?'

I wished she could understand my plight. Her agony was justified, but I couldn't do what she wanted.

'I have to make it quick. I can't miss my flight,' I said and opened the door.

'Dravya,' she called out as I stepped out of the car. 'I love you,' she said, her voice quivering. 'Can't this stop you?' she asked smiling through her tears.

I kept gazing at her. How could she love me so much? She deserved someone better.

'This is the last flight to London. I cannot miss this. Thank you for dropping me,' I said.

We finally moved towards the entrance; she couldn't accompany me beyond this point.

'Is there nothing that can stop you?' she said, almost begging.

'Please Khushi, not again,' I answered.

'Shh... Don't say a word,' she kept her finger on my lips. 'I know you won't stop. I love you, but that doesn't mean you have to love me back. It's okay... I understand!' she said softly.

While people were suggested not to travel until it was absolutely necessary, here I was, leaving the country for a girl.

Khushi embraced me for the last time. As if she had a very strong feeling that I wouldn't be returning.

'Dravya,' she took my name softly.

'Yes!' I whispered.

'You have to come back,' she said with a lot of conviction. 'If you have no reason to return, make me one,' she added.

'I will…' I answered, my voice faltering.

I picked my bag and walked towards the queue. I didn't know whether Khushi was still there, looking at me, or was she gone. I didn't want to turn back. I didn't want to face Khushi's tears.

Maybe what I was doing with Khushi was wrong, but if I stayed with her, I would never keep her happy. I could never love her the way she loved me. In fact, I had never loved her. I just loved the girl for whom I was catching this flight.

People may fall in love multiple times, but I had risen in love, only once. I couldn't imagine living without her, forgetting her. Nobody could stop me from meeting her now, not even a global pandemic.

If this is indeed the end, I would rather spend my final moments in the arms of my beloved. She changed me, my life, my world, everything…

'Dravya…' I heard somebody calling me. It seemed to be Sid's voice. Was he here?

I turned back and stepped aside from the queue.

Sid was standing beside Khushi, with his hands resting on the knees, panting, trying to steady his breath.

What was he doing here, I wondered.

'We need to talk,' he got straight to the point.

I was startled. I was not expecting him here. I looked at my wristwatch to indicate subtly that I couldn't give him much time.

I looked at Khushi. Her eyes were glued at me. Why was Sid panting? Was he alright? My eyes hovered around. Simmi was supposed to be with him. Where was she?

'Call me, Sid. I'm going inside,' I said, pointing at my watch. 'Is Simmi okay?' I enquired.

'Yes, she's okay, but I need a minute,' he replied firmly.

I had no choice but to walk towards him.

'You're flying to London? Seriously?' he asked.

I was silent. He calmed down as he saw a helpless look on my face.

'Are you sure?' he asked.

'What the hell is wrong with you guys?' I looked at Khushi and then at Sid. 'Why are you asking me the same question, again and again?'

'Because we care for you, Dravya.' Sid kept his hand on my shoulder. 'You've gone crazy. I can't let you do this. You can't board this last flight. Have you thought what this means?' he added.

'You guys can go home. This is the last flight and I can't miss this,' I said and lifted my bag. 'Nothing will happen to me, Sid. Don't worry.'

'People are dying all over the world. Why don't you understand! This is suicidal,' he said, snatching my bag.

Sidharth Jhunjhunwala, my best friend, had been with me through thick and thin, rendering unconditional support. It was his strong concern for me that brought him to the airport, amidst all the chaos.

'Dravya,' Simmi came to us.

'Simmi, you okay?' I looked at her.

'Yeah, I'm alright. Took a while to park,' she replied. She added, 'Come on, Dravya! You don't have to do all this. Sid, do something! We can't let him go.'

'Guys, no one can stop me,' I said in an assertive voice. 'I've made up my mind.'

'Dravya, please... She's gone. There is nothing left to hold on to. What do you expect after three years?' Simmi said softly.

'I still love her,' I said.

'And what about her?' she asked.

'I guess she has the same feelings for me,' I said.

'You guess? You're catching this flight on a guess?' she seemed surprised.

'This is my love story, Simmi,' I said, with conviction.

Shagun had stood at the same place three years back, to move on in her life. In spite of all the efforts which Dravya had made to stop her, she hadn't budged. It was precisely at that moment where their love story took a pause. But Dravya's affection for Shagun did not.

'I'm done convincing this idiot,' Simmi shouted at Sid. 'Will you tell him?'

'I have been trying since the day he told me his plan. How do you expect me to stop him? What should I do?' Sid responded in a dejected voice.

'Guys, stop it!' I shouted at both of them. 'I'm catching this flight and no one can stop me.'

Deep inside their heart, they all knew that once I made up my mind, there was no looking back. Obstinacy and determination were in my genes.

I knew what they were saying was practical, but love knows no logic. It is an innate force which propels you to overcome all obstacles, transcend all boundaries and claim what belongs to you.

'We all are going home, Dravya,' Simmi said. 'With you. I'll get the car,' she said looking at me.

'I'm not going anywhere,' I said, now getting irritated.

'And how will you return?' they asked.

'I'll figure it out,' I said.

'India is going under complete lockdown for a minimum of three weeks. You'll get stuck there,' Sid yelled.

I didn't want to tell the girls about the lockdown, but Sid spilled it out. I shouldn't have discussed this with Sid.

'Don't say this to anyone,' I said looking at both the girls. 'It's highly confidential.'

'I'll get the car for the two of us then, Sid,' Simmi said in anger. 'It's useless explaining anything to him now.'

I knew Simmi cared for me. She didn't want me to go. She was still expecting for something to happen so that I could stay back. After all, she was my dearest friend after Sid. How could she let me risk my life? Even I would try to stop her if she was in my place.

'I should leave now. It's time,' I said.

I hugged Sid and opened my arms for Simmi. She came running to hug me. 'I hope you are right.'

'I am,' I whispered. 'I don't have her address, please arrange that for me.'

'I'll message you. Tell her that we miss her,' she said.

'Sure.' We let go of each other.

'I am sorry for everything.' I apologized to Khushi.

'You kept me in the dark. How could you, Dravya? Have you thought what will happen if the situation gets worse and the lockdown is extended? How will you get back?'

'I will manage,' I replied.

Khushi came forward to hug me as well. But her eyes were brimming with resentment now.

She was playing with the ring I had put on her finger on our engagement day.

'What all will you manage? You're going to meet your ex, leaving everything behind. You're leaving me. You don't care about our engagement. You don't care about your friends. You knew about the lockdown and yet you never shared it with me. You're catching the last international flight and risking your life, just to meet your ex! What else are you hiding from me?' she said everything in a single breath.

I stood there, speechless. I knew every word that Khushi uttered was true and yet I could not let her sway my mind now. From this point, there was no going back for me.

'Here!' she took off her ring and gave it to me. 'If you are sure of what you want to do, I think this makes things pretty clear for me too.

'But tell me, all this drama... for what? Are you even sure Shagun is Covid positive?' she asked.

I nodded, tears rolling down my cheeks.

Down the Memory Lane

I closed my eyes, hoping to slip into a deep slumber on the flight. Unfortunately, I kept tossing restlessly. Sleep had deserted me, owing to my anxious heart.

I was dying to meet Shagun. She was fighting for her life. I yearned to tell her that I was still in love with her. Even today, I could walk an extra mile to bring a smile on her face.

I had full faith in my relationship. I knew her love for me can never change. I know her very well. Even though we left each other, we could never be separated. We were strung together by our unconditional affection.

I didn't fight for her back then. I blame myself for everything. I was wrong! I should have listened to her and stopped her from leaving the country.

I am sorry for everything, Shagun. I wish circumstances were different then. I wish, I wish and I only wish…

Unable to sleep, I called the flight attendant.

'Can I have some water, please?' I politely asked.

'Sure sir, I'll just get some for you,' she responded, smiling.

Within a minute, she came back with a glass of water for me.

'Would you like to have some more, sir?' she asked after I was done.

'No, thank you,' I said and gave her the empty glass.

Due to this unprecedented outbreak, people were avoiding travelling overseas, but I was risking my life to meet Shagun.

I had no plans to catch this flight until I came to know that Shagun was Covid positive. I know my friends were right. I mean, catching the last flight in this outbreak without any idea of how I would return. All this sounds stupid and filmy, but it was happening with me.

Coronavirus was serious and lethal, and so was my love.

As I was ruminating over the complexities of my life choices, I saw an air hostess coming out of the cabin. She seemed familiar to me. I thought I knew her from somewhere.

'Tanya?' I called her. She looked up at me.

'Yes,' she raised her eyebrows.

'Are you Tanya Agarwal?' I asked.

'Yes!' She was still confused. I pulled my mask down.

'Oh my god! Dravya Seth? Is that really you?' She was startled. 'I don't believe this is you.'

'I don't believe either.' I smiled. We shook hands.

'How are you?' she asked.

'I'm good! What about you?' I responded.

'Even I am good,' she replied.

'You look amazing. It has been such a long time since we last met,' I said. I was pretty impressed by her transformation.

From a reticent and shy girl, she had emerged into a strong and confident woman.

'Thank you!' She blushed.

'Girl power, huh?' I said looking at her badge which was pinned near her shoulder. 'Not bad.'

'Yeah, girl power.' She chuckled.

'So how's everything with you?'

'All well, you say, how's life?'

'In love with my job,' she said.

'Yeah! I can see the glow on your face while you speak,' I said.

'Really?' She laughed. 'Life is in the sky.'

Our conversation inevitably shifted to coronavirus. What else could one talk about? That was the hottest topic for every human being. How the virus was spreading from Wuhan to almost every country in the world.

We talked for a little while. I was downing my second cup of coffee when Aashi, another flight attendant who had joined us by now, asked, 'So, you live in London?'

'No,' I replied. 'I live in India.'

'Then why are you catching the last flight to London?' she asked.

'Actually, I'm flying for a girl,' I said.

'For a girl?' Aashi responded, looking at my ring. 'Your wife or fiancée?'

'She must be very lucky,' Tanya added.

'I was lucky to have her,' I said.

'Was?' Tanya had noticed.

'Yes, was!' I replied.

'And the ring?' she asked.

'It's my engagement ring, which is useless. I just called it off,' I kept the coffee and said, taking off the ring. 'It ended a few hours ago at the Delhi airport,' I said looking at the ring.

'At the airport?' Both of them looked at each other.

'Yes!' I smiled.

'So who's in London?' they asked.

'My ex,' I replied.

'Your ex? You're flying for your ex?' Tanya's eyes almost popped out and Aashi's mouth remained half opened.

'I don't know what to say,' Tanya said, with a tone of amazement.

'Neither do I,' Aashi added.

'You guys look awestruck. Are your guys confused?' I asked, smiling. I was enjoying this now.

'Yes,' both of them said together.

'Have you guys ever fallen in love? True love makes you do extraordinary things. That's what I am doing. I'm doing this for Shagun,' I said, in an attempt to clear their confusion.

'That's you ex's name?' Tanya asked.

'Yes!' I responded.

'And your fiancée, I mean ex fiancée?' she asked.

'Her name was Khushi,' I replied.

'Hmm, so she broke up because she knew you were flying for your ex?' Aashi asked.

'No, she realised I didn't want this relationship, and I had hidden crucial information about her,' I said, looking at the confusion reflected on their faces. 'I had to, for the country. I couldn't tell her what's going to happen in a couple of days.'

'What's going to happen?' Tanya asked.

'I can't tell you,' I was not sure if I could.

'Come on, Dravya! It's just a couple of days. We will find out anyway.'

She was right. I couldn't hide it for too long and I was bursting with anxiety myself. So I announced suddenly, 'India is going to be under a nationwide three-week lockdown Monday onwards.'

Tanya gasped, and Aashi started giggling. 'What a joke! Now come on, tell us the truth!' Aashi said.

I smiled, even as Tanya glared at Aashi, almost chiding her, 'Believe him; he doesn't need to lie or joke about this.'

Aashi became serious and asked innocently, 'But how would he know all this?'

'Because his father is the Home Minister of Uttar Pradesh!' Tanya said softly but the impact of the words showed on Aashi's face.

'You're his son? I mean, wow!'

'Fortunately and unfortunately, yes!'

Tanya came to her rescue and asked me instead, 'So that's why you wanted to be on this flight so desperately?'

'I had no choice. I couldn't let Shagun down. Not again.'

'So you got engaged to Khushi and then realized that you love Shagun?' Aashi asked.

'No, I always loved Shagun,' I said.

'Does she know that you are coming to London for her?' Tanya asked.

'We broke up three years ago,' I replied.

'Then, why are you risking your life?' Tanya wondered.

'I am going because Shagun is probably Covid positive,' I took some time to say that. My eyes were teary once again.

'What?' Tanya almost spilled her coffee. Aashi had just sipped hers, which she gulped in slowly.

'So this is why you caught this flight?' Tanya asked softly.

'Yes,' I replied.

'But what do you mean by probably?' she asked again. 'You're not sure?'

'No, it's not confirmed, but I feel she is.'

My heart knew Shagun was Covid positive. I had to be beside her. I couldn't leave her alone, not this time. No matter what happened to me, I had to do this. I didn't want to lose her again. Our love is immortal.

'You have changed a lot,' Tanya said.

'Yes!' I smiled. That's how I could respond to Tanya's statement. Shagun had really transformed me. I have turned into a new leaf.

'You know what, Dravya? I want to know everything about Shagun. I want to know how you met her, how you fell in love with her. I know your school-days stories. Do one thing, start from the day you saw Shagun for the first time,' Tanya said excitedly.

'From the first day?' I took off my specs.

'Yeah, from the first day. We have plenty of time. We don't have to catch any flight.' Tanya winked and started laughing.

A ripple of laughter reverberated around us.

I started. 'Okay then. It all started when I was still waiting for him.

Love at First Sight

March 2011

I was still waiting for him in my car. Fifteen minutes had passed and yet there was no sight of him.

'Why aren't you taking my calls? Where the fuck are you?' I snapped at him as soon as he received my call.

'Just five minutes,' he replied and got off the line.

I lit a cigarette and pulled in a few puffs. Though I was a second year student in Banaras Hindu College, studies were never my cup of tea. While other students were found in the classrooms, I belonged to the playground and the pubs.

'Baba,' my driver called me.

'Yes!' I responded.

'Sid is taking time,' he said.

'So?' I asked in irritation. Sid was clearly getting onto my nerves now.

'We are on the wrong side, Baba. Shall I park the car on the other side?' he asked, in a submissive voice.

'What?' I burst out laughing. 'What's wrong with you, Sunil? I am Dravya Seth. Nobody has the audacity to do anything to me. No traffic policeman can touch me or my car. You drive a car with a red beacon light on top. Why do you even have to worry about anything?'

'Traffic rules, Baba,' he replied.

I rolled my eyes in annoyance. *Rules were for the common men, not for VIPs like us. We were meant to lead, not to follow.*

Finally, Sid stepped out and walked to me. He was well-dressed, donning one of his best outfits, and came with a debonair smile on his face.

'Hey!' Sid guffawed.

'Few minutes more and I would have left,' I said annoyingly.

'You can never do that,' he said.

'You said it was urgent, that's why,' I replied.

'Yes, it is urgent,' he said, stepping into the car.

'Vasanta College,' he said to the driver.

'What?' I shouted at him. 'You have called me here for this?'

'Yes!' Sid winked at me.

'What the fuck is wrong with you, man?' I yelled at him.

'What?' Sid reacted.

'Are you serious?' I glared at him.

'Yeah…' he replied casually.

'Get off my car,' I pushed him in anger.

'It's really urgent.' Sid laughed.

'What is so vital in Vasanta College?' I shouted.

'You know well.' Sid kept laughing.

'Alright, fine, fine, fine… Vasanta College,' I said to my driver.

My car took the last turn. I was not ready to believe what my eyes were seeing. 'Oh shit!' I looked at Sid. 'Is this what you have got me here for?'

'It's amazing.' Sid laughed and looked down at his shoes, primping his jeans accordingly.

The students were immersed in their Holi celebration and the ambience was filled with colours. I hated colours and I hated the way people were behaving while playing with colours.

The car slowed down and was parked on one end after we reached Vasanta College. Sid stepped down the car and I said, 'Make it quick.'

'You're not coming with me?' Sid asked.

'No,' I replied.

'Why?' He sounded disappointed.

'I hate colours, you know that,' I said.

'As you wish,' Sid said and walked away.

Sid was madly in love with his girlfriend Simmi. I knew everything about them.

My phone rang and Sid's name flashed on the screen. 'Are you sure you don't want to come?' he confirmed.

'Damn sure!' I asserted confidently.

'Simmi wants to meet you,' he said louder. His voice obscured in the loud laughter of the gathering.

'Why? Tell her I'll meet her some other day.'

'She wants to play Holi with you,' I heard him say.

'Holi? No way, Sid!' I made myself absolutely clear.

'Sid is crazy, Sunil,' I said after I disconnected the call. 'He's really crazy. Simmi wants to play Holi with me and Sid is insisting that I should be there,' I said.

'Be with your friends, Baba. You are blessed with such caring companions. Do not neglect their presence and importance. Life is not only about cigs and black dog. Relationships are also important,' he responded.

I sat quietly in my car, musing on his words and trying to make sense of what he was trying to explain to me.

Should I get down from my car and join them? Maybe I can try something new for a change.

I got down from my car and called up Sid to ask where he was. He was outside Chocolates. It was a famous confectionery shop near Vasanta College.

I was heading towards Chocolates when somebody threw a handful of dry colour powder in the air and shouted, *'Holi hai...'*

I squeezed my eyes and moved my hand to make space in the crowd. The bright red and blue colour had formed a strange splash design on my branded Nike T-shirt. I was about to reach Chocolates when a bike stopped right in front of me and blocked my way.

A girl took a few steps towards it and sprang on to sit on the bike. I moved aside. While she sat on bike, her skirt scaled a few inches up and revealed her magnificent thighs.

My eyes were glued to her sexy and well-shaped thighs. I tried to catch a glimpse of her face, but she vanished in a jiffy. Her sheer presence was so magnetic.

What was happening to me? Why couldn't I take my eyes off her? Come on Dravya, this is not you! It may seem like a brief encounter, but it felt as if I had known her for eternity. I longed for her. I wish time had stood still.

'Dravya...' I heard someone calling me.

'Dravya...' The voice came again. I was too busy trying to relive the moment to notice someone calling me. I could only see her long silky hair which blew in the air.

'Dravya!' Sid shook me when I didn't respond.

'I want her,' I said softly.

'What?' he asked.

'I want her,' I said little louder.

'Who?' He asked again.

'That girl,' I pointed at her.

'Oh, that girl on the bike?' He sounded surprised.

'Yes!' I confirmed.

'She's Shagun, Simmi's friend,' Sid replied.

'You know her?' I looked at Sid.

'Yeah, somehow...' he replied.

'Great!' I hugged him. My happiness was immeasurable.

'Come on, let's go! We should be going home now.' Sid kept his arm across my shoulder and we walked towards the car. I dropped Sid and then headed back home. While I was on my way, my mind was fixated on one name.

Shagun. There was something hypnotic about this name. It cast a spell on me. Was it the magic of love?

I wanted to meet Shagun. I don't know why, but some strong force was pulling me towards her. *Should I talk to Sid? Or should I talk to Simmi? No, they will laugh at me. What will*

Simmi think about me? Sid will surely laugh at me. How should I talk to them? I was perplexed.

I wanted to meet Shagun, but I didn't want Sid and Simmi to know about it. Was that possible? No, Dravya. It was not possible without involving them.

'Sid?' I called him up.

'Yes!' he replied.

'Where are you?'

'You just dropped me home,' he replied.

'I want to meet you,' I said.

'What's wrong with you? Don't tell me you really want to meet Shagun.' He kept laughing.

'No, not at all,' I said quickly.

'Then why do you want to meet me now? You just dropped me a few minutes ago.'

'Shut the fuck up, Sid!' I hung up. I knew Sid would laugh at me. I shouldn't have called him.

I wish he could understand the plight of a restless heart. I sighed.

A Rocky Start

When you want something, the entire universe conspires in helping you to achieve it.

This wisdom of a great author was apt for my life. While I was unable to meet Shagun, the universe decided to take over my love story.

On a Sunday, when Sid wanted to meet Simmi, he tagged me along as well. Unwillingly, I had to accompany him, but who would have known what was waiting for me out there!

It turned out that Simmi had come with none other than Shagun.

'Excuse me,' Shagun came and I shifted to make space for her. She sat next to Simmi and I sat beside Sid.

'Dravya,' Sid called me.

'Yeah,' I replied without looking at him. I was engrossed in my cell phone.

'Do you know her?' he asked.

'Who?' I pretended.

'Simmi's friend?' he asked.

I looked at her and then replied, 'No!'

'You don't know her, Dravya?' Sid guffawed.

'No... What's wrong?' I looked at Shagun again and said.

'You know her, Dravya,' he said, with a mischievous smile.

'What are you talking about, Sid?' I asked once again. I was genuinely unaware of what he was hinting at.

'Think, Dravya, think properly,' he insisted.

'You can't recognize her?' he asked. 'She's the girl you fell in love with. Remember, her sexy thighs? You fell in love with her thighs,' Sid said and started laughing.

'Sid,' I looked at him, enraged. But it was too late. Shagun's face turned pale. She had overheard our conversation and was too shocked to respond.

'Excuse me,' Shagun stood up with her eyes wet with tears and walked away. She must have been so appalled by this conversation and was surely filled with anger and grief.

'Shagun,' Simmi called out and went after her.

'What the hell, Sid! Have you gone crazy today?' I yelled out in anger.

'What did I do?' Sid pulled Shagun's burger and started adding ketchup. He began to eat.

'You shouldn't have done that,' I said softly.

'Oops, sorry!' Sid kept the burger back and shifted the tray to where it was.

'I'm not talking about the burger, Sid,' I said irritated.

'Then?' He wiped his mouth using the tissue paper.

'You know well,' I said.

'Hmm... Sorry.' He nodded casually.

'You should say sorry to Shagun,' I said.

'Sid,' Simmi roared in rage.

'Where's your friend?' I asked Simmi.

'She went home weeping,' Simmi shouted at Sid.

'What did I do?' Sid asked.

'You made her cry,' Simmi shouted.

Simmi called up Shagun, but she didn't answer. Sid defended himself by saying that he was only messing with me and had no intention to offend Shagun. As I imagined those precious tears dripping from her face, my heart sank.

That night, I was lying on my bed, unable to sleep. My mind was lingering somewhere around Shagun's weeping face. I couldn't think of anything beyond her beautiful and snivelling face.

I didn't know what to do. Shagun was ravishing. I wanted to gaze deeply into her bewitching eyes. Her lustrous lips were so beguiling. Her green kurta with the black border only enhanced her beauty. My eyes wanted to see her again. My heart wanted to beat only for her now.

'Sid, how is Shagun?' I whispered as we were in class.

Sid raised his eyebrow slightly.

'You didn't ask Simmi about Shagun?'

'No,' he whispered.

'Why?' I muttered.

'Why should I?' he responded with a tone of indifference.

'Sid?' I couldn't believe it, and gave him a tough look. He didn't utter a word. I kept glaring at him and then looked in front at the professor who was taking our class.

'She's fine,' he whispered after a second and I turned to him. 'I spoke to Simmi last night about her.'

'Hmm…' I said.

'Want her number?' Sid asked me.

'No!'

'Take it,' he said softly.

'No.' I shook my head but finally lost control over my smile.

'Dravya,' Sid's whisper rose. 'You liked her?'

'No,' I tried to hide my smile again.

'You're blushing, Dravya,' he said notoriously.

'No!' I said looking straight at him this time.

'She's single,' he said. 'I asked Simmi.'

'No, Sid.' I smiled.

'If you want, I can help you,' he offered.

'I don't want your help,' I said.

'Fine,' he said. Then he slowly took out his cell phone and started typing something. My cell phone vibrated.

'I've sent her number to you. Keep if you want, or else, delete.' I looked at him and blushed.

'Don't worry, I won't tell anyone,' Sid said.

I smiled.

Should I call her? Or message her? But message her what?

I thought as soon as I reached home. I lay down on my cozy bed and opened Sid's message in which her cell phone number was written. I read her number again and again. I loved reading her number. I couldn't wait to start this relationship. With this pleasant thought, I closed my eyes and drifted off to sleep.

Hangover

'One more,' I said to the waiter after he kept the first peg on the table.

'Sure, sir!' he said and left.

Sid and I were sitting in a bar where I was boozing. As usual, Sid was enjoying his soft drink. I ordered for a chicken tandoori after the waiter got another drink for me. I relished my drink and the soulful music.

'How can you drink so much, Dravya?' Sid asked.

'Why, what happened?' Then I turned to the waiter and said, 'One more!'

'This is your fourth drink,' he commented.

'So?' I asked.

'Check please,' Sid said to the waiter.

'Drink, please,' I vetoed.

'Sir?' The waiter was bemused.

'Uff… Do what you want to,' Sid responded.

I was on my fifth drink when my mind diverted towards Shagun. I wanted to meet her. I don't know what, but there was surely something bewitching about Shagun which was pulling me towards her. I was desperate to know her.

Our first introduction was through her tears, which I could never forget. She went home weeping because of me. I had to apologize to her.

Should I call her today after I get home? Or should I talk to Simmi first?

Talking to a girl is easy, but talking to that girl who you love is the most difficult task. It's like you are walking on thin ice. One wrong word and everything can be ruined. I didn't want to say anything that could potentially hurt her. After all, I was in love for the first time.

'I think I should talk to Shagun,' I said.

'What?' he asked.

'I mean, message,' I added.

'What are you saying, Dravya?' Sid sounded surprised.

'I think I should message her,' I said a little louder.

'Message who? Shagun?' he asked.

'Yes!' I confirmed.

'What will you message her?' Sid laughed.

'Stop laughing! I want to apologize. She went home crying because of you, remember?'I said.

'That's an old story. Simmi cleared everything. Do you know people babble after getting high? You're drunk, let's go home,' Sid said.

I wanted to apologize, but Sid thought I wasn't serious. He thought I was saying all this because I was blitzed. Now who would explain to him how serious I was for Shagun.

'Let's go,' Sid said again.

'Yeah,' I said and killed my shot, bottoms up.

Once home, I walked straight up to my room. The room was unlit but the brightness of my cell phone illuminated my face. I was still wondering whether I should message her or not. I was staring at the screen of my phone which flashed the word, "Hi".

"Should I press the 'send' button or not?" I asked myself.

Without deliberating further, I took a leap of faith and pressed the button. My heartbeat accelerated like never before. I kept my phone aside and closed my eyes. But how could I sleep? My heart was waiting for her reply.

'Hello?' I said in my drowsy voice.

'Dravya?' It was Sid.

'Yes,' I said, chafing my eyes.

'Are you coming to college or not? You're late,' he asked.

'No,' I replied.

'Why?' He sounded worried.

'I don't feel like coming today,' I said softly.

'Hangover?'

'No…' I interrupted. 'Stop annoying me,' I said and hung up.

Anxiously, I checked my phone, but was disappointed. I wondered if I should have mentioned my name in the message. The suspense of this situation was unnerving.

Should I message her again with my name? No, she'll think I'm craving for her. Ahh... What mess have I created for myself?

I regretted my decision of texting her. I was thinking of ways to mend the situation when my mother entered the room.

'Dravya, you didn't go to college today?' she asked.

'No,' I replied. She drew the curtains aside. 'Mom?' I shouted.

'What happened, Dravya?' she asked and sat next to me.

I didn't reply. I didn't want to talk to anybody. Shagun hadn't replied to my message. Her lack of response was bothering me.

I was about to cover my face with a pillow when I heard a message beep on my cell phone. I quickly removed the pillow and my eyes opened at once. I jumped over my phone in excitement and my heart hovered like a free bird in the sky. But my enthusiasm was shattered upon reading the notification.

"Dial *123#3# to set *mora piya* of Rajneeti as your new caller tune only for Rs. 30* Offer valid till today. Terms and conditions apply."

Was this really love or just infatuation? Why was I so desperate to receive her message?

In an hour, breakfast arrived in my room. I left my bed and dawdled towards the breakfast kept on the table. I bounced on the couch, snuggling myself. I looked over my breakfast and then looked at my mom.

'What?' she asked.

I didn't want to eat, and here, she brought me aloo paratha with butter on them. I wish I could tell her that I wasn't hungry.

I took the glass of orange juice in my hand and sipped slowly. "Aloo paratha, not bad," my heart awed.

Love? I still wonder how people fall in love?

I was going crazy since I had not received any reply from Shagun till now. What happens when couples fight? I had seen Sid and Simmi brawling. How do they manage? Do they also go insane like me?

I was still wondering about all this when I heard Sid's phone ringing. I took the phone in my hand. It was Simmi. 'Sid, your phone is ringing,' I said and kept the phone back.

'Who is it?' His voice echoed in the washroom.

'Simmi,' I replied.

'I'm coming,' he said.

I didn't want to wait. After seeing Simmi's call, Shagun's memories returned to my mind. I received the call. I wanted to ask her about Shagun.

'Hello,' I heard from the other side.

'Hey, honey!' I said.

'Dravya darling, how are you?' She laughed.

'I'm good! So how's your friend?' I asked.

'Who friend? Shagun?' Simmi giggled. 'She's fine. Even she must have reached home by now. All okay with you? Why are you asking about her? Are you serious?'

'Serious as in?' I pretended I hadn't understood the question.

'You have feelings for her, right?' she confirmed.

'Maybe.' I laughed.

'Maybe, huh?' Simmi stretched her last word. 'But be careful daring, she's a very demure and simple girl. You two have strikingly opposite personalities. I wonder how you will connect. But nevertheless, she is beautiful,' she said.

Yes, she's splendid indeed. And maybe, her enchanting beauty was pulling me towards her. Should I tell Simmi that I had messaged Shagun last night when I was sloshed and she didn't reply? She may probably understand.

'I heard you are hitting for college secretary?' she asked. Her voice interrupted my chain of thoughts. I answered in the affirmative.

'I don't think it's a good option right now,' Simmi suggested.

'Don't worry, nothing will happen. I know how I've to take care of everything.'

I gave Sid his phone. I took the remote in my hand and kept surfing through music channels. It was then that my phone beeped. My heart swung and I felt I was on a roller coaster. It was her message. It was just a question mark.

I looked at Sid. He was busy talking to Simmi. 'Dravya,' I replied to her question mark. Another message beeped. It was again a question mark.

'Dravya Seth,' I replied. Another question mark arrived.

'Are you joking?' I asked.

'What do you think?' she replied.

She really didn't know me! I was startled.

Sid hung up the phone and said, 'What are you smiling for?'

'Nothing.' I looked at him.

He looked at my phone. 'Somebody sent you a joke?'

'She replied,' I said.

'She? Who?' Sid kept his phone on the table.

I gave him a broad smile and lifted my eyebrow twice.

'Hold on a sec! Shagun? You finally messaged her?' His voice was filled with excitement.

'Yes! I messaged her last night'

'What are you guys talking about?' he asked inquisitively.

I sat beside Sid and made him read my conversation with Shagun. He laughed at the three question marks. It was difficult for him to digest that I was talking to a girl.

Sid called up Simmi to tell her what was happening between me and Shagun. None of them could believe that I had approached a girl. Even I couldn't believe that I was actually doing this. Even in her messages, there was something riveting about her which made me stick to my phone.

The first thing I did was to apologize for the mess that Sid had created on the first day we saw each other. She graciously accepted my apology, which made me fall in love with her all the more. Our love story began, with just a question mark.

Election Extravaganza

"Vote for Dravya, vote for Dravya, vote for Dravya…"

My name was reverberating in every corner of Banaras Hindu College. A popular student belonging to a political family was participating in BHU elections. The manifesto was released, widely distributed and scattered all over the campus. My fellow competitors wanted to defeat me at any cost.

The elections weren't easy. The student union was banned abruptly when large-scale violence paralysed the university campus on 20 February 1997. A student was killed during a blatant display of firearms while an election rally was underway at the amphitheatre ground. The Vice-Chancellor of the university, Dr Y.C. Simdhari, ordered an indefinite ban on the union elections within the campus, and rightly so.

The existing student council was going to get revamped with a more democratic outlook. The election process involved a three-step process. Thus, all the students were given an opportunity to elect their representatives at the department level. The elected representatives then elected candidates at the faculty level and later on, they chose the candidate to become secretary.

The election was about to take place after about fourteen years. The agenda was to form a council, not a union.

Even though the process was revamped, the dirty games of politics stayed. It can never be fair and transparent.

My phone buzzed. It was Shagun. I'd asked her whether she had reached home or not. It'd been more than a month since we started talking. We had developed a warm connection over messages, even though we had not spoken on call.

'Where are you?' she asked.

'College,' I replied.

'You're still in college?' she texted.

'Yes, we are still working,' I replied.

'And where's Sid?' she asked.

'He just moved out,' I replied.

I had started developing feelings for Shagun. My romantic feelings were transpiring through messages. How do I explain? It was amazing!

'Come on, guys! What else can we do to win this election?'

I looked around and asked my comrades. They all were working very hard to support me. I was excited to emerge victorious. No doubt, I wielded a lot of power and prestige in the university, but winning the election would add another feather in my cap. I wanted to achieve this new frontier of excellence.

I lit a cigarette in the classroom and the discussion went on about the campaign. Plans were put on and off the table. The competition was fierce and we ought to put our best foot forward.

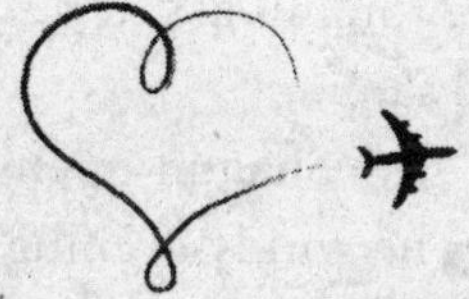

A Pleasant Coincidence

'Is it true that your opponents are forming an alliance to defeat you?' Simmi asked.

'Yes,' I replied.

I stirred my coffee and lifted the mug to take a sip. I took the first sip and said, 'Banaras Cafe serves you the finest coffee in the city.' Sid and Simmi looked at each other in amazement.

'Dravya, should I ask you something? What will you do about the alliance?' Simmi asked.

'Nothing is going to work. We all know the new rules of the election. It will rupture the alliance. Don't worry guys. I've been working on every clause from the very first day. There is nothing to worry about,' I said in a voice brimming with confidence.

'Oh, that's why you planned this evening outing to relax with us? I mean, a surprise evening outing.'

'No, I have done this for Shagun. She didn't want to meet alone, so I said you guys are also joining,' I said.

'And then she agreed?' Sid asked.

'Of course!' I said.

'Then where is she?' Simmi asked next.

"There she is!" Sid said.

I turned back and saw Shagun opening the cafe's gate and entering with a smile. The windy evening swung her hair, along with numerous wind chimes which adorned the cafe. The serene music played by those wind chimes welcomed her for me.

'Hi, guys!' She joined us.

'Hey,' I offered her to sit.

'Thank you,' she sat on the plush couch. 'Sorry, I'm a little late. Evening traffic, you know.'

'No problem, even we just came,' I said.

'Just?' Simmi looked at me.

'Yeah, so?' I blinked at her and sniggered.

'Anyways, what will you have?' Simmi asked Shagun.

'Coffee will work,' Shagun said looking at the cups on the table.

'Good choice,' Sid said, signalling at the waiter.

My eyes went to Shagun after every few seconds. I couldn't take my eyes off her. Our conversation went on and we spent quality time with each other. I was charmed by her beauty and demeanour. Ecstatically, I kept sneaking glimpses at her admirable features.

'So, Shagun, how's your college going?' Sid asked her.

'It's going good, thank you for asking. What about you?'

'Same, just a little busy,' he replied.

'Busy? In some project?' she asked.

'No... Actually, you can say yes. Winning elections is always a project.'

'I'm not sure. Did you hear about the alliance?' Simmi said.

'What about the alliance?' Shagun turned to Simmi.

'Forget it, guys. We haven't come here to talk about the election,' I said.

'An alliance has been formed to defeat Dravya,' Simmi said.

'Really?' Shagun turned to me. 'You never told me.'

'What should I say? You're not interested in my college elections. In fact, you dislike politics. So there was nothing to tell you.'

'But how come an alliance?' Shagun said after a pause. 'There are some new rules. Something along the lines of step by step, I think? How is that possible?'

'Yes, I did, but it is politics, you know! It can never be pristine,' I said.

'Don't tell me Kaushal Yadav is the mastermind,' Shagun said.

'You know him?' Sid asked, keeping his cup on the table.

'How would I know him?' Shagun giggled.

'I don't know, I just thought,' Sid said softly.

'No,' Shagun said smiling and sipped her coffee.

Smitten by Dravya

Shagun's face had a new colour that day as she couldn't stop smiling. She had spent a lovely evening with her friends, especially Dravya. With every interaction, her prejudices about him were melting away. She had begun to admire his raw and unfiltered version.

As she returned home, her phone started ringing. To her amusement, the phone screen flashed Dravya's name.

'It was fun today,' he said.

'Yeah, it was fun,' she said and kept the phone. Even though they were brief moments of interaction, it did not fail to make their hearts flutter.

On the other side of the receiver, Dravya was also revelling in the rhythm of Shagun's voice. Cupid had started working on both of them.

Pride or Ego?

'How's your campaign going, Dravya?' Dad asked me at the dining table.

'Good, Dad!' I replied.

'Will you win?' He asked.

'Of course, Dad! How can you doubt my excellence? I am invincible,' I asserted myself in a loud voice.

'You're over-confident,' he said.

'Come on, Dad! All of us, sitting at this table, can confidently claim that tomorrow, the sun will rise in the east. This is a universal truth which has stood the test of time. So will be my victory. Dravya has never seen the face of defeat. And, he will never see it,' I said, beaming with pride.

My dad looked at my mom and smiled. 'Just look at your son. He knows how to riposte.'

'He's learning from you,' she added smiling.

'The chapatti isn't hot,' I looked at the maid. 'You know I don't like this careless attitude and negligence,' I shouted at the old, frail-looking maid who was about to serve me shahi paneer.

'I'll just get some, Baba,' she scurried to the kitchen.

My mother was stunned by my response. She asked, 'Why you are so short tempered?'

'He's my son. Fire is in his flood,' Dad added.

'So?' Mom asked. 'Does this give him permission to be so rude?'

'Yes,' I said boldly. 'I can do anything.'

'Baba, hot chapatti.' The maid served me.

'I don't want to eat,' I said and stood up fiercely. The chair fell backward as I stomped off to my room.

'Just because the chapatti was not hot?' she asked.

'Yes!' Shagun and I were chatting on the phone.

'You need to have control on yourself,' she said in a soothing voice.

'I try, but…' I started, but she interrupted me in the middle.

'But what?' Shagun jammed in.

'But I always fail,' I took a moment to say it.

'Practise yoga. It's very beneficial.' She suggested.

'What are you saying, Shagun?' I sniggered.

'There's nothing to laugh, it works.'

'Really?' I kept laughing.

'Uff… It's futile to explain to you. You can continue being an irascible.' She pretended to be angry and kept the phone down.

I had a wide smile on my face. Now, I was convinced that I was irrevocably in love with her. Her smile, her face, everything…

'I am proposing to Shagun,' I informed Sid excitedly.

When? Before the election or after?' He asked.

'Before,' I replied. 'I want her by my side officially and see my victory.'

'Dravya and Sidharth?' The professor pointed out to us.

'Yes professor.' We stood up.

'I know you have to discuss a lot about elections, but this can happen after my class. Both of you are creating a lot of disturbance. I believe you may not benefit a lot from my lectures, but I won't let you become a hindrance in the learning process of the others,' he said, in a sarcastic tone.

Sid was a bit apologetic, but I remain undeterred.

'You guys please walk out if you want,' he said angrily.

Sid was about to apologize for both of us when I shouted, 'We'll walk out.'

'Dravya?' Sid looked at me in dismay.

'Let' go, Sid! Let's go,' I packed my bag.

'We're going,' I said little louder.

'Sir, we are sorry. We'll stay,' Sid apologized.

'No Sid, we won't! We are leaving,' I said, fuming in anger.

'Make it quick, whatever you want to do,' the professor said impatiently.

'I'm waiting for you outside.' I bustled out.

Sid packed his bag in a hurry and followed me.

'Is there anyone else who wants to leave the class?' the professor yelled.

In the next five seconds, some other students picked up their bags and walked out with me to express their solidarity.

'This is my power,' I walked to the professor and said, looking into his eyes.

'You are an incredible leader.' Sid patted my shoulder in anger.

'What do you mean?' I asked.

We were not out of the class.

'Nothing, see you tomorrow,' he said and walked away.

I took a deep breath and closed my eyes, thinking what just happened.

The same night, I was lazying around my room after dinner when I heard my phone ringing. It was Simmi. I checked and kept the phone back. I didn't want to talk to anyone. It rang again, and once again, it was her. I finally received the call reluctantly.

'Sleeping?' I heard her asking.

'No, tell me?' I replied.

'What happened today shouldn't have happened. You need to control your emotions, Dravya. Don't let them overpower your sanity,' she said in a comforting voice.

'Hmm… Sid told you?' I asked.

'Yeah, we met today,' she replied.

'He left college early.'

'He came to my college,' she said.

'Really?' I guffawed.

'Shagun is very disappointed,' Simmi said.

'Shagun? How does she know?...You told her?' I asked.

'We were together when Sid came to our college,' Simmi said.

'So he told her?' I asked.

'Yes!' she replied.

'Great! And what did she say?' I was curious.

'It was your fault,' Simmi said softly.

'Shagun said this?' I asked.

'No Dravya, I'm telling you this. Where will you go with this snobbish and aggressive attitude? What will you do?'

'It wasn't my fault. I didn't ask the entire class to pack up and walk out with me.'

'Your fault was that statement to the professor,' Simmi pointed out my mistake.

'I don't give a damn, Simmi. It just happened. You all have to understand this,' I shouted at her.

'Sid is also very upset,' Simmi said after a pause.

'I don't care,' I said, fuming.

'You do! All of us know that,' Simmi said and I hung up, irked.

First, when Simmi saw Sid waiting for her outside her college, she was shocked. She thought he had come there to surprise her. But the moment she hugged him, she realized something was wrong. She felt a bit different while he hugged her back. His low tone confirmed her hunch. Later, they sat in a cafe nearby and Sid told them everything that had happened in college. God knows what's wrong with Sid? Why does he have to share everything with Simmi?

Simmi suggested that I must apologize to the professor, which I refused to do. Why should I apologize to the professor? We were sitting in class. It was he who pointed at me saying, "You guys can walk out if you want." I didn't ask any student to walk out with me. Why should I be sorry? It was the professor's fault.

I called Shagun, but she didn't receive my call. I kept the phone aside and tried to sleep. I closed my eyes and everything that had happened in the afternoon came rushing back to my mind, especially what Simmi had said.

You need to control your emotions, Dravya. Don't let them overpower your sanity.

The Game-changer

In every election, there is only one weapon which is the most formidable and puissant amongst all. Something that has the power to turn the tables. And that's money. The game-changer.

Arranging funds during elections is the most difficult task for any politician. The more the funds, the higher the chances to win the election. 'You don't have to worry about funds, Dravya,' Sid said.

'Exactly, I have my dad with me. Why worry?' Another drink arrived on the table. 'One more,' I ordered.

'Sure sir!' The waiter nodded and walked away.

'And now, the largest funds in the history of BHU will be raised,' I boasted.

'How much?' Simmi asked.

'Don't ask that,' Sid scoffed.

'You know?' Simmi turned to Sid.

'Obviously, Dravya told me a few days ago,' Sid replied.

'And when were you going to tell me?' Simmi asked.

'Today.' Sid laughed.

'Yes, yes, tell me,' she adjusted herself to listen to me. 'So what's the plan?' She gave her best smile.

'Remember I always told you guys that their alliance will break? And I also said that since rules are new in this election, I'll do something which will ensure that I win by a sweeping majority.'

'Yes! Now, I am really excited to listen to what you're going to say next,' Simmi took her shot bottoms up and said.

'I'm buying the representatives,' I said.

'What? Very good, Dravya.' Simmi was startled.

'But I don't understand one thing. You already have your party outside of college, and eventually, you will join your dad and get involved in state elections. Why waste money on BHU elections? Either you win or you lose here, doesn't matter, right?'

'It does, Simmi. I want to be the most influential youth of our state. I strive to leverage the BHU elections to build a successful career. We are planning to buy the representatives to seal our victory, but we couldn't buy all of them because some are not in our favour. They are true devotees of Kaushal Yadav. There will be some exceptions. But I am leaving no stone unturned to win this.'

I meticulously explained my strategy to Simmi. She was overwhelmed with happiness.

'You must have told Shagun, right?' Simmi asked me.

'Shagun doesn't know anything. She knows nothing about buying representatives,' I informed her.

'Really?' Simmi's eyes widened. 'I don't believe this. But why?' Simmi asked me.

'You know her very well. After all, she's your friend.' I smiled.

'Yeah, she's sort of *satyawaadi*. Too naïve to understand the ways of the world.' Simmi sipped her vodka.

'She's very innocent,' she added.

'This is why I fell in love with her.' I couldn't help but blush.

'Really?' Simmi laughed. 'Then, convey your love to her.'

'I will! In fact, I will propose to her now.' I gulped the alcohol and said.

'Now?' Simmi looked at Sid.

'You're kidding, right?' Sid sounded startled.

'No, I am serious!'

'Guys, don't do this. You can't propose her this way. You are sloshed.' Sid stopped us.

'Let's do it. Trust me, she'll accept my proposal,' I said in a confident voice.

'I know her better. She's my friend. She will never accept this way. Get yourself together first and then you can,' Simmi said.

'I'm just squiffy. I'll get sober by the time we reach Shagun's place. I don't want to hear anything. We're doing this now. Let's go!' I stood up.

'May the lord be with you.' Simmi stood up and swung her handbag on one shoulder. We settled the bill and walked out of the bar.

The Proposal

We were on our way to Shagun's house when I called her up and asked her to come to the park behind her house.

The moment that I had been ardently waiting for was finally here. I asked her to reach the park in fifteen minutes. To make this special, I bought a rose for her.

'You're drunk. Don't get close to her,' Sid said as soon as the car stopped near the park.

I got down from the car adjusting my clothes. 'I won't. You guys are not coming?'

'No, we'll wait in the car.'

Simmi leaned her forehead on Sid's shoulder and said, 'All the best!'

I smiled and started walking towards the park. A slight cool breeze was rustling the leaves, making them fall to the ground one by one. My skin shone under the bright sunshine. The fragrance of the fresh flowers filled me with immense joy. Unable to control my excitement, I gave her a call.

'Where are you?' I asked.

'Right behind you,' she said, in her melodious voice.

I turned back and was left astounded.

Shagun was wearing a pink chikankari suit with a white chiffon dupatta. Her face was radiant and her hair messy. She looked surreal.

'You're looking beautiful, like always.' I sighed.

Shagun looked down smiling and pinned her hair behind her left ear.

'Why have you called me here at this time?' She looked up at me.

I took out the rose which I had been hiding in my shirt and took a step closer to her. She looked at the red rose and I looked into her eyes. Her eyelashes blinked and a smile brightened her face. She looked up at me and said nothing. Her lips may have been closed, but her eyes conveyed everything. I blushed and my heart knew her reply.

My heart raced in exhilaration. I took a step closer to her and said, 'I love you.'

Shagun's smile disappeared and she moved a few steps back. She covered her nose and mouth with her dupatta. 'You're drunk!'

'Don't come near me,' she said pointing at me and stepped back.

'What's wrong with you, Shagun?' I asked softly.

'What's wrong with *me?* What the hell is wrong with you, Dravya? You've come here to propose to me... this way? I'm going,' she said in anger and turned around to walk away.

'Shagun,' I followed her.

'I don't want to hear anything,' she said and scampered towards the exit.

'Shagun, wait!' I caught her hand.

'Don't touch me, Dravya,' she shouted and released her hand.

She tried to release her hand, but couldn't. My anger took the better of me and I held her tighter. She resisted, but to no avail.

'Dravya…' I heard Simmi's voice. I saw Simmi and Sid running towards us. They saw me holding Shagun's hand forcefully.

'What are you doing, Dravya?' Simmi asked.

'Leave her hand. What's wrong with you?' Sid said.

'You guys stay quiet. It's between me and Shagun. I love her and I can do anything. You guys wait in the car. I am coming,' I said to them.

'Enough, Dravya, leave her!' Sid said and got over me. He caught my hand and tried to loosen my fingers. I caught Shagun's hand even tighter and kept gazing at her.

'You're hurting me,' Shagun said, looking into my eyes.

'What do you think? With power and force, you can impose your love on me. No! Never!' Her voice shivered. 'I'll never be yours.'

Her eyes didn't blink at all. I could now sense her anger behind her tears. My heartbeat almost stopped and the fear of losing her engulfed my soul. Our confrontation caught a lot of undesirable attention. As I got back into my senses, I released her from my grip.

'Today, you have fallen from my grace. I hate you, Dravya Seth. I hate you!'

She took a few steps back, turned around and started walking.

'Shagun...' I said again.

'Shagun,' Simmi called and ran after her.

I fell on my knees with the rose in one hand. Sid came to support me, but I pushed him aside in anger. The petals of the rose withered away. I opened my arms and screamed, 'Shagun...' Simmi turned back, but Shagun didn't.

Dravya has never seen the face of defeat. And, he will never see.

As I saw Shagun walking away from my life, I saw the face of defeat for the first time.

The Fight

'She doesn't want to talk to you,' Simmi said. I was in my class, sitting on the professor's desk with my foot on his chair, talking to Simmi over a call.

'You told her that I want to apologize?'

'Yes,' Simmi replied.

'And then too she doesn't want to talk?'

'No,' Simmi said softly.

'Shit man! I screwed up everything yesterday.'

'You shouldn't have caught her hand and forced yourself upon her. I have a huge regard for your love for her, but you should respect her consent. Love cannot be enforced. She told me that you have hurt her pride and dignity. There is no turning back for her now,' Simmi said after a pause.

'She told you that?' That upset me a great deal.

'Yes,' Simmi sounded quite low.

'She's not taking my calls either,' I said exasperated.

'Don't worry, Dravya. I'll explain everything. Give her some time,' she said in a comforting voice.

'Hmm...' I replied.

'Anyway, where are you?' Simmi's tone changed to cheer me up.

I said I was in college and I wanted to spend some time alone.

As I was sharing my agony with Simmi, I heard a loud knock on the door, which startled me.

'Hello, Dravya!' Kaushal called out.

'Kaushal Yadav?' I mumbled.

'What? Kaushal Yadav is there? What is he doing there at this time?' Simmi panicked.

'So, Kaushal, what brings you to me?' I kept the phone on the desk and asked.

'I heard you're buying representatives?' He entered the lecture hall with his friends. 'Is it true?'

'Who told you?' I asked.

'Some of my friends whom you approached and they were not for sale.'

'Tell me, Dravya. Is it true?' He walked closer to me.

'What if I say yes? You think you can defeat me?' I gave an arrogant smile.

'One hundred percent,' he said.

'How?' I asked.

'That's not the question. How will you save yourself from us? This is supposed to be the actual question. Well, I've been waiting for this opportunity.'

In a jiffy, Kaushal pounced and hit me on my head with the lower portion of the gun. It was so quick that I couldn't defend myself. In an impulse, I caught his neck and rammed him against the wall. My outrage took the better of me and I pressed his neck hard, almost to kill him. There were deep furrows in his brow.

His eyes turned red and watered. He was suffocating and was trying to escape, but I didn't let him. 'Now what, Kaushal?' I grunted.

In the next moment, he hit me again on my head with the pistol. I could not take this blow and almost fainted. Everything blurred. Blood was all over my face and I couldn't see Kaushal's furrowing face any longer. He hit me for the third time.

I could now hear the police sirens blaring. I tried to get up, but couldn't. My vision was slowly becoming darker. As I was slowly moving towards unconsciousness, my mind wandered to the pleasant memories of Shagun. I longed to feel the warmth of Shagun's embrace.

I heard a few footsteps coming closer to me. I tried to open my eyes and see who it was, but failed to do so. Gradually, I slipped into a deep slumber.

The Reunion

I slowly opened my eyes and found myself lying on a bed. I was in a hospital.

'Mom?' I tried to get up, grunting.

'Don't get up, son.' She laid me down.

'Ah, my head,' I squeezed my eyes shut in pain.

'Sid, call the doctor!' Mom said to him.

I was lying on the bed and looking at the ceiling fan, recalling what happened with me. Everything came back to me; the bloody fight with Kaushal Yadav, the anger, the revenge.

'So, Dravya, how are you feeling?' the doctor asked after examining me.

'Good,' I mumbled in pain. 'Just my head...'

'Oh, don't worry. It's because of the stitches. It will be fine in a couple of weeks. Mrs Seth, can we please have a word in my cabin?'

'Yes, doctor,' she panicked.

'Please don't worry, Mrs Seth. Nothing serious! It's just some formalities regarding the discharge.' He smiled.

'Doctor?' A nurse entered. 'The police is here, they want the patient's statement.'

'Not now, please. He just woke up. They will ruffle my son by asking uncomfortable questions,' Mom said.

'Don't worry, Mrs Seth, I'll take care of the police,' the doctor said and walked out of the room.

'How're you feeling?' Sid asked smiling after the door was shut. I smiled as I could barely speak.

'Twenty-six stitches, man! It must have been gruelling for you.'

'Sid,' I moved my hand calling him.

'BHU fight, police, how?' I tried to frame my questions through a few words.

'I called them. Simmi informed me about you being stuck with Kaushal Yadav and his gang. Honestly speaking, it wasn't my idea. I informed the police, but it was never my idea.'

'Then?' I asked, but deep down, I knew the answer.

'Shagun,' Sid said after a pause.

'Shagun?' I mumbled.

Simmi and Shagun were together when I was talking to Simmi. Shagun suggested that we must involve the police. As it was a high profile case, the police will take quick action.

'You should be thankful to Shagun,' he said.

'Hmm...' I wiped my tears.

I was now thirsty for revenge, but winning the election was my first priority. I had to figure out how I was going to deal with Kaushal Yadav. Sid had the names of all the boys who had cornered me that day. They were thirty-three, including Kaushal Yadav. I decided to not involve my dad.

I wanted to say something to Sid, but before I could, somebody knocked at the door and entered. It was Shagun. She was breathing heavily.

'Hey, how are you?' Shagun asked me.

'Good,' I said softly. I couldn't speak, but I was excited to see Shagun in the room.

'You know why I'm here, right?' she asked.

'No.' I nodded. My heart was jumping in excitement.

'I am wearing the same suit that I wore when we met last. I want to restart from where it almost ended.' Her tone changed. She was serious. 'I have something for you,' she said and moved her hand into her handbag.

She took out a rose and said, smiling, 'I know it's not the same rose, but it's similar.'

She came closer to me and said, 'Dravya.' I could feel my heart stop.

'I love you. But this can't happen. We can't be together. I want a simple life. I am an ordinary girl who wants to spend her life with an ordinary boy, who cherishes simplicity. You are the son of an influential politician. Our worlds do not intersect. We both want different things in life,' her voice shivered.

'Shagun,' I said softly and moved my hand to call her.

She bent down to hear me. Her hair bestrew on my face, which she pinned quickly behind her ear. 'Your lifestyle, my lifestyle. Okay?' I mumbled.

'So no more alcohol? Politics?' she asked.

'No.'

'You'll do this for me?'

'Yes!'

I caught her nose and pulled her gently close to me. I kissed her forehead and whispered softly with tears in my eyes, 'I love you too.'

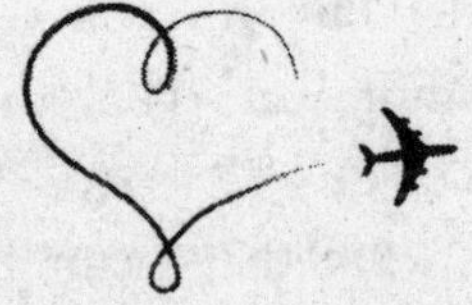

Turning Over a New Leaf

When you fall in love, your entire existence revolves around that one person who matters to you the most. You long to be in the company of your better half. And that's what I wanted.

Shagun's presence had filled my life with immense happiness.

I had withdrawn my name from the university elections. I was no longer in the competition. It left a lingering guilt in my heart. But, it is believed that every ominous event has a silver lining. Life eventually works out for the best. With Shagun by my side, I was prepared to take a leap of faith and rediscover myself.

With time, my life came back on track. I started going to my college. I gave a false statement to the police that I didn't know who had assaulted me. I gave up on the elections and forgave Kaushal Yadav for his misdeeds. This made him victorious.

'I never expected this from you,' Sid said. 'Everyone is disappointed.'

'I can understand. But love changes you. In my case, Shagun changed me.'

'Love changed you? But, do you realize how people are talking about your withdrawal? They think you are scared of Kaushal,' he said.

'People will think what they want to think, Sid. Do you really care about them? I don't!'

Giving up all these things was not easy for me. I would have never given up if Shagun wouldn't have asked for it. The gangster of BHU had metamorphosed into an empathetic individual who was ready to think beyond himself.

'Sir, your cold coffee with ice-cream,' the waiter said and kept the glass on the table. 'Ma'am, your strawberry mojito,' he added.

'Thank you,' Shagun greeted the waiter with a smile.

'You're welcome, ma'am. Enjoy your drink.' He smiled and took a leave from our table. I kept staring at Shagun. It was our fifth official date.

'What?'

'Why did you say thank you? He's doing his job.'

'Dravya, this is basic common courtesy. Besides, you don't lose anything by making someone smile,' she said excitedly.

'What? He's doing his job and I'm paying for the drinks. Where did "thank you" come from? Instead, he should be thankful to me,' I said brusquely.

'Forget it, Dravya. You are an MLA's son. You won't understand the value of little things. We all have our little follies.

Baby, this is just the way you are. How do I explain it to you?' She raised her eyebrow, forming curves on her forehead.

'What? What did you just call me? Did you call me "baby"?' I smiled.

'What? Nothing!' She blushed and looked down at her drink, circling the straw, smiling.

After lunch, we headed back. My car stopped near the park and Shagun looked at me to bid farewell. We got down from the car. 'Should I go?' she asked.

'Will you stop if I ask you to?' I replied, winking at her.

She once again looked down, her cheeks glowing crimson red. By that time, dusk was upon us and Shagun's face gleamed under the sunshine. I couldn't take my eyes off her.

I took a step closer to her and gently pulled her to me. She closed her eyes. I kissed her on her forehead. She smiled.

'Bye and I love you,' I whispered in her ear.

'Hmm…' She nodded without looking up and left. I kept gazing at her until she vanished from sight.

The same night, I was having dinner with my family. Everyone was quietly enjoying the meal. There was an uncanny silence in the room. Finally, my father spoke, 'You shouldn't have done that. You withdrew your name from BHU election. You didn't tell me who hurt you. You even lied to the police. What's wrong with you?'

'I have moved on, Dad. I want to make a fresh start. Explore myself beyond politics,' I replied.

'After wasting a huge amount of money?' he said quickly. 'I'm very disappointed with you, Dravya.'

'I'm sorry Dad, but I really changed my mind. I'm no longer interested in politics.' I finally spoke to him, mustering some courage.

'What?' He looked at my mom. 'What's wrong with your son?'

'How am I supposed to know?'

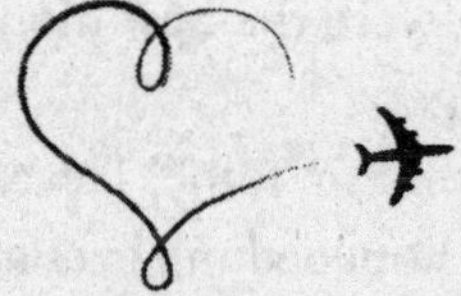

Dashashwamedh Ghat

'Hey,' I said as soon as Shagun stopped in front of me.

'Hey,' she gave an entrancing smile. She was wearing a red patiyala suit which had white coloured leaves printed on it. Her red sandals matched her dress and she looked exquisite, like always.

'Just one thing is missing. May I?'

'Hmm...' She looked down.

I slowly pulled out the wooden stick holding her hair in a bun and messed them a bit. Her long hair fell free. 'Now, it's perfect,' I said.

She looked into my eyes and smiled. We got into the car and I drove to the Dashashwamedh Ghat. We had planned to see the Ganga *aarti* together. I booked a boat for the two of us, which took us to the other side of the ghat. We spent some time there and then returned to the boat. Shagun's hair swayed with the breeze, which she kept controlling.

'Leave it, it's beautiful,' I said looking at her.

Her waving hair touched my face and I closed my eyes, feeling her aroma. I leaned backward for her hair to touch every part of my face. Those were the best moments of my life, which I was sure to never forget.

Shagun kept her hand on mine. Her warm touch refilled my happiness to the brim. I opened my eyes and sat up straight. The sunset changed the colour of Ganga and Shagun's face to fire. My eyes rolled down to Shagun's lips. I kept staring at her smile and moved closer to her. My lips were an inch away from hers when she closed her eyes. We kissed each other for the first time.

For the first time, Shagun nestled in my arms. We looked at each other, smiling. We were so close that I could feel Shagun's breath on me. We looked up at the sky and gazed at the birds flying above us.

Soon, we came back to the Dashashwamedh Ghat and sat down to see the aarti, which was about to begin. People teemed, looking for the best spot where they could sit and take part in the aarti.

Shagun held my hand and we witnessed the beautiful aarti. Later, we also bought diyas, which Shagun lit. Her smiling face glimmered with diyas and we floated them in the river together.

We sat there for some more time, dabbling our feet in the river and feeling the love, and then I dropped Shagun near the park.

'Did you like it today?' I asked.

'I loved it. It was one of the most beautiful evenings of my life.'

'What?' My dad looked perturbed. 'Why do you want to do this?'

'Education is important, Dad,' I said.

'Since when? It was never important for you until now. You were always interested in politics. What's happening to you? ' He was startled.

My graduation was over and I had decided to begin with my Master's. I was still not interested. I was going only for Shagun.

It is amusing that when you're in love, you tend to respond more to the instincts of your heart.

My parents didn't want me to go. They wanted me to stay in Varanasi and expand our family business. We had hotels, liquor factories and the largest coal depot in the state. They wanted me to look after all these and carve my niche in politics.

'Fine,' my dad said and I stopped. 'Go wherever you want to, but remember one thing. One day you have to return to fulfil your responsibilities. You can't run away then.'

'Thank you, Dad,' I said. My vibrant face couldn't conceal my excitement. I was ecstatic.

Delhi Diaries

People enjoy life in Delhi, but I was homesick.

I was missing Varanasi, the campus of BHU, the Ganga aarti and everything which was related to my native town. It took me some time to adapt to the fast rhythm of the capital. But, I had to for Shagun's happiness. I was so deeply in love with her. My dad even bought a flat in Delhi for me.

Mithu and his father were the caretakers of my flat. When I shifted to Delhi, he was sent here. He worked as a liftman for additional income.

'What took you so long, Mithu?' I asked after he entered the flat.

'Bhaiya, the restaurant you sent me to, they made me wait for very long,' he said and kept the parcel on the dining table.

'And my credit card?' I asked.

'Oh, I just forgot,' he bit his tongue and said. 'Here,' he took out the card from his wallet and gave it to me.

'So Mithu is carrying wallet in Delhi, huh?' Simmi reacted after she saw him keeping the wallet in his back pocket.

'So, how much cash Mithu is carrying in his wallet?' Shagun raised her eyebrows twice and asked smiling.

'Thirty rupees, didi,' he replied.

'Here, keep some more cash,' Shagun took out a few hundred and fifty-rupee notes from her purse.

'No,' Mithu hesitated. 'Bhaiya,' he looked at me.

'Keep it, Mithu,' Shagun shook her hand along with the notes.

'No, please, I can't.' He hesitated.

'Bhaiya,' he looked at Sid.

'Keep it, Mithu! Your Shagun di is giving you,' she said in her soft tone.

Mithu took the cash and kept it in his wallet. He folded his hand to express his gratitude and left.

'Why would you do that?' Sid asked after Mithu was gone.

'He's just fourteen years old,' Shagun replied.

'We pay his parents for whatever he does here. What's wrong with your friend, Simmi? She always does this.' He turned to Simmi.

Before Simmi could reply, I stood up and said, 'Let's go and have our lunch.'

'Can I ask you something?' Sid looked at Shagun after we settled down on the dining table.

'Yeah, sure,' Shagun replied.

'Why do you always do this? All this charity sort of things, why?' Sid asked.

'We don't need any reason to do good,' Shagun replied smiling. 'Try doing it yourself, Sid. You will feel good.'

'If you keep squandering your cash this way, then Shagun Jewellers will inundate and soon drown,' Sid laughed and passed the bowl to Simmi.

Shagun didn't reply. Instead, she just smiled and concentrated on her meal. The tension in the atmosphere made everyone uncomfortable. Shagun chose not to escalate this trivial matter and diffused it with silence.

Our lives took a new turn in Delhi. Shagun and I started pursuing our MBA from International Management Institute and Sid and Simmi entered FORE School of Management. Even though our paths diverged, we ensured that our friendship remained stronger than ever.

IMI broadened my worldview and profoundly influenced my personality. It was radically different from BHU. While IMI had a very intensive academic culture, seasoned professors and ambitious student fraternity, BHU was home to me. I was known and loved by everyone. I had my moments of alienation even in this vibrant culture. I wished with all my heart that this management school was in Varanasi.

My train of thoughts was disrupted when Shagun called out to me. We were in the library as Shagun wanted to read more on social entrepreneurship.

'What are you doing?' She was startled and moved away after I pulled her.

'What?' I said softly.

'What?' She lifted her eyebrows.

'Come close to me,' I whispered.

'Here?' she said softly and looked around.

'Yes!' I nodded.

'Can I get my books issued now?' she whispered.

'No! I want a kiss first,' I said softly.

'What?' Shagun's eyes popped out. 'Here? Have you gone crazy, Boo?' She added.

'Sort of.' I smiled.

'Leave my hand,' she said softly and pulled her hand back.

'Give me a kiss first.'

The silent library froze, and for the first time, I found the library worthwhile. Shagun came close to me and whispered, 'Close your eyes.' I did what she asked me to.

Shagun kept both her hands on my chest and said softly, 'No way, Dravya Seth,' and laughed lightly.

The moment I opened my eyes, she pushed me and chuckled. Her delightful chuckle was so loud that it echoed it the silent library. Every face turned to us and kept staring as if we had come to steal from the library and we were caught by the police.

The middle aged, bald librarian looked at us from the top of his thick spectacles and gestured, 'Shh...' He then, pointed at the board saying "SILENCE PLEASE". I quickly started pretending to look for a book on the other shelf. I didn't want to look at people gazing at us.

Shagun engaged herself by looking for her books and soon the havoc settled down. I looked at her from the corner of my eye but shifted my gaze on the books quickly when I saw a few students still staring at me.

Shagun got her books issued and I kept pretending to ruffle the pages.

'Boo,' she called me softly. 'I'm done, let's go!'

I didn't respond. I wanted her to know that I was sulking. Sometimes, it's good to pretend sulking and tickle your love, right?

'Boo,' she whispered again. 'Let's go!'

I ignored her and pulled a book out of the shelf and flipped few pages, pretending to read. I didn't turn back.

'Boo,' she whispered and I felt her aroma closer to me.

She slowly took the book from behind and lifted her toe to reach me. She pecked me on my cheeks from the back and ran out of the library with her books.

'Boo,' I screamed and ran after her.

Once again, the entire library turned to us and I heard the librarian, 'Shh.'

'What do you expect from next week?' I asked Shagun when we were sitting near the window, watching the sky pouring down.

'I can't say anything right now. Let's see,' she replied softly. 'I just hope our campus placement tests and interviews go well for both of us.'

'It will go well,' I kept my hand on hers and said.

'Hmm...' She looked at me and smiled.

'Your eyes...' I said.

'What?' Her eyes glittered.

'They are gorgeous,' I said.

Shagun stole her eyes away and looked down. A portion of her hair fell over and covered her face slightly. I pinned her hair back and gazed at her beautiful face.

'Look up,' I said softly.

She raised her eyes after a few seconds and again stole away her gaze from me. It was almost five years of our relationship and Shagun was still shy in front of me. Not always, but in some aspect, she was. I moved close to her and kissed her forehead. She closed her eyes and I kissed them. I cuddled her nose with my nose, which made her smile. Shagun embraced me in her arms and I kissed her.

I could feel Shagun breathing heavily. Our kiss lasted for a long time. I rolled down to her neck and took a long deep breath. Her aroma... it was enchanting. I slowly kissed Shagun's neck and felt her fingers exploring my back. Her scent nipped every part of my body. Shagun surrendered herself in my arms and hugged me so tight that I could feel her heart racing.

The melody of the falling raindrops added a magical touch to our inevitable union.

Campus Placement Jitters

Our campus placement was going to start from Friday onwards. Simmi was curious to know our future plans and goals, especially if we did not end up with a job in the same city.

"We'll figure it out," was Shagun's reply. And I said, 'Let's see what happens first.'

The last bit of warmth was drawn off by the setting sun. Shagun and I were going back home. I was still thinking about what Simmi had asked us.

'What if we don't land up in the same city?' I asked Shagun.

'Then I'll quit and live with you, whichever city you go to,' she said quickly.

'No, Boo. This is not what you wanted. You always aspired to work for a good MNC. You wanted to be a successful corporate professional,' I said in a tone of dismay.

'Then, what is the option?' she said.

'I'll quit,' I said, pondering.

'No, you don't have to do that.' She got very anxious.

'We'll see after all the interviews. I'm sure we can get in the same city like Simmi and Sid got,' she smiled and said.

'I love you,' I said after a moment.

'Hmm...' She quickly looked down and kept her beautiful smile.

An Unexpected Phone-call

It was going to be a wonderful day. The sun was light and black clouds hovered overhead. The breeze was gentle and cold. It was probably going to be the first rain of 2016 in Delhi. The entire IMI was silent, like always.

We all were buckled up and our faces gleamed with confidence to impress the interviewers. It was going to be the first round. We all sat quietly with fluttering hearts, waiting for our turn.

'Boo,' Shagun whispered. 'Are you nervous?' She raised her eyebrows.

I took a deep breath and said, 'Probably... What about you?'

'Me too. But no matter what happens, we are always together.' She smiled.

'Dravya Seth?' I heard my name being called out.

'Yes sir!' I responded, startled, and freed my hand from Shagun's.

'You're next after him,' the faculty member pointed at the guy going in.

'Yes, sir.' I nodded. I looked at Shagun and smiled.

'All the best,' she whispered.

'Thank you,' I said softly.

I was still waiting for the guy to come out when I felt my phone vibrating. I took out my phone and checked. I looked at Shagun and smiled.

'Who is it?' she asked.

'Mom,' I whispered.

'Must have called to wish you luck. Take it,' she said.

'Yes, Mom,' I received the call and said in my cheerful voice.

The weather outside worsened as there was roaring thunder and lightning. I felt they were for me. Everything froze for a second and soon it started raining. In that moment, I froze too. My smile disappeared and my eyes halted at Shagun.

Seeing my smile vanish so suddenly, her smile was wiped off too. 'What happened?' she asked.

'Dravya Seth,' the faculty member called my name.

I winced, aghast at the news I had just got. I stood holding the phone to my ear.

'Dravya Seth,' he called my name again. 'Get in!' he added.

'Boo, what happened?' Shagun pulled my hand down. 'Is everything okay?'

'Dad, my dad...' My voice shook.

'What happened to him?' She took the phone from me and disconnected the call. 'Is he alright?'

'Dravya Seth, you want to go in or should I send someone else inside?' The faculty member said in annoyance.

'Boo, please tell me what happened,' Shagun said in her low tone.

'He's been shot,' I said after a pause.

'Dravya Seth?' He called me again.

'Shut up!' I turned to him and shouted.

The entire gathering in the lobby turned to me. It was so loud that even the interviewers stepped out to check what happened. 'What's happening? Is everything okay here?' One of them asked.

I looked around at people gazing at me. 'I'm sorry,' I said to the faculty member, trying to keep my cool. 'I'm so sorry.'

I turned to Shagun. 'I have to go.' My eyes blinked continuously while saying.

'Yes, you should definitely go,' she said. 'Do you want me to come along with you?'

'No, you stay here,' I said and dashed out of the lobby.

I was running across the campus towards the exit gate in the rain when I heard Shagun calling me. I stopped and turned back. Shagun was breathing heavily like I was and she too was drenched in rain.

'What happened?' I screamed.

Shagun ran to me and stood in front of me, panting.

'You have an interview. Why are you wet?' I asked.

'Because I told you we'll get wet in this rain together,' she replied, trying to hold her heavy breath.

'Oh Boo!'

'And I don't give a damn to this campus selection. As long as you're standing by my side, I don't care about anything else,' she said with conviction.

'But you wanted this. This is your dream,' I said.

'Not any more. Your dreams are mine now and I want only you,' she said quickly.

'And this campus placement?' I asked.

'I just want to be with you. Whether in Delhi or Varanasi. Wherever you go. I just want to follow you,' she said, holding my hand.

'But Boo...' I said.

'But what?' she asked.

'I'm coming back,' I said.

'We can come back together. Let me come with you,' she said.

'I have a reason. How will *you* convince the management about your absence?' I asked.

'I don't know. We'll figure it out after coming back here,' she replied.

'No, this is not happening. I can't let you ruin your career this way. You can't do this.' I insisted.

'Boo, please!' she requested.

'My dad has been shot. I have to be there. Please don't mess anything more for me,' I said in a low tone.

'How will I live here?' Her voice broke down. 'Without you, how?'

'I'll come back soon,' I said.

'Nothing will happen to my dad. I know he's a fighter.' I added.

'I hope so...' she responded.

'I'll come back after everything gets normal there.'

'So you want me to stay here alone?' she asked.

'You have to,' I took her hand in mine and said. 'I am certain that you will nail your interview today.'

My phone rang. It was Sid.

'How's uncle?' He came straight to the point.

'Admitted in the hospital,' I replied.

'Two bullets in his chest?' Sid said.

'Yes,' my voice shook. 'How do you know?'

'Dravya, the news is out everywhere. He's an influential politician.'

'The situation is critical,' he added.

'What? Who told you?' The ground beneath my feet seemed to have shaken.

'My dad, he's in the hospital,' he replied.

'I'm going back,' I said. My voice was quivering.

'I'm catching the next available flight too,' he said before hanging up.

'Boo...' Shagun grabbed my hand. She took a step towards me. She went up on her toes and gently held my nose in her forefinger and thumb. Pulling me closer, she kissed my forehead. She nuzzled my nose with hers and caught my hand again. She looked into my eyes and said, 'I love you, I love you so much.'

I nodded, with tears in my eyes and released my hand to walk away. I could feel the howling gales in Varanasi. Nothing was more important than catching the first flight which would take me to my dad.

My car crawled, making its way on the crowded road. Our party flag was everywhere. I kept squirming, trying to make out what was happening and how far the hospital was.

'How far, Sunil?' I asked frantically.

'We have almost reached, Baba, but this crowd... This is unbelievable!' he responded.

'Vishal Seth has been shot today, this was also unbelievable.' I wondered.

'Should I get down?' I asked.

'No Baba, anything can happen here,' he warned.

'Sunil, do something,' I howled in agony. 'I can't stay here anymore.'

Sunil rolled down the glass and bawled, honking at people, asking them to clear the way for my car. The gathering was huge and the chanting for the party and my dad was louder than ever. Nobody was listening. The thought of losing my dad filled me with immense dread and with every passing second, my blood was turning colder.

'I'm going,' I said and opened the door.

It was so crowded that I could barely open the door properly. I resisted and somehow managed to wiggle and get out of the car. I hobbled through the crowd and kept hustling myself towards the hospital. I looked around at the buildings and realized that

I was almost a kilometre away from the hospital. I kept sliding myself and jostled to make my way. This was the only way to reach my dad.

I finally saw the hospital building and my heartbeat accelerated like never before. Cars, buses, tyres were burning everywhere. I kept slogging, fighting back and finally reached the hospital.

'Baba,' I heard a voice. It was Vijay who scurried towards me.

'How is dad?' I asked as soon as he came closer.

'Still in the operation theatre,' he replied.

'DSP!' I shouted as soon as I saw him outside the OT. I pointed and wagged my fingers to call him.

'Just a constable at the entrance? Who do you think is admitted here? Your dad?' I burst as soon as he stood in front of me. My ruffian self was back.

'Who is he?' he asked Vijay.

'I'm Dravya Seth, Vishal Seth's son,' I shouted.

'Oh,' he quickly responded and turned active.

'Take all your men outside and guard the entrance. My men will take care of everything inside,' I ordered.

'But...'

'Pradhan uncle is still the commissioner here?' I crossed him.

'Yes,' he replied.

'I'll talk to him. You do what I'm saying. Any information about the shooter?' I asked next.

'Not yet, we are tracing. It can be anyone,' Malik replied. Malik was one of the most powerful members of our party. 'We have election in February,' he added.

'It can be someone from the liquor mafia,' Vijay said. 'Something related to coal, hotel...'

'It can be anyone,' I said pondering.

'Call the commissioner, ask him to interrogate every mafia of the city and state,' I said to Malik. 'Tell him Dravya is in Varanasi.'

In the meanwhile, doctors walked out of the OT and I rushed to them.

'Doctor, how's my dad?' My voice shook.

'Sethji is out of danger now,' one of them replied smiling.

'Thank you, thank you so much,' I clasped his hand and bowed my forehead to touch them.

'Can you do me a favour, please?' he added.

'Anything,' I looked up to him and wiped my tears.

'The city is burning... Please do something. See the enormous gathering outside the hospital. This is a hospital and it is not going to help us. Please?' the doctor said.

'Yes, Baba. Only you can do this now. People will only listen to you in Sethji's absence,' Malik said.

'Me?' I hesitated. 'I've never done this. I've never addressed this huge a gathering. They don't even know me. How can I?' I mumbled.

'Do it, son. Even we have to get home,' the doctor said and walked away with his team trailing him.

'How do I start...?' I said softly.

'Like you used to in BHU,' someone from the gathering said quickly.

'Okay, I'll try,' I said after thinking for a few minutes. Everyone was right. Only I could stop the ruckus. After all, I am Vishal Seth's son. I channelized my inner energies to connect with people and assured them that their beloved leader would recover soon.

The people were mesmerized by my words. They showed their affection and gratitude for me by chanting my name. At the end of the speech, we folded our hands and observed some silence to pray for dad's well-being.

In those moments of silence, I became conscious of how I was meant to step into the shoes of my great father.

Shagun's Dream Came True

'Dad is fine now,' I said to Shagun over phone.

'Yes, I know that,' she said in her cheerful voice.

'How?' I smiled.

'You were live on every news channel. They are still showing you,' she added.

'Are you still watching me?'

'Yes, do you want to hear?' She increased the volume of TV.

'You're still in the mess?' I asked.

'Yes,' she replied. 'I wanted to see you and we have a television only in the college mess.'

'News channels, I tell you. They got another breaking news of the day.'

'Sid reached?' she asked.

'Yes, he is sitting beside me.' I turned to him and smiled.

'You took him and you left me alone here,' she sounded a bit displeased.

'I didn't get him here. He came on his own. I told him not to come, but he didn't listen to me,' I said.

'He has certainly proved that he's your best friend. He has always supported you through thick and thin. You are very lucky,' she said.

'You are right. He is not just my best friend, but my brother,' I kept my hand across his shoulder and said.

'Yeah, your bro,' she giggled. 'Where is uncle now?' she asked.

'He's okay. They shifted him to the room an hour ago,' I replied. 'It was a hectic day. The city experienced so much of chaos and mayhem.'

'Yes, I spoke to my dad today. He mentioned about the riots and the damage caused to public property. The city was on high alert. He even told me that the government was going to impose a curfew, but they waited after your speech in which you requested people to bring peace in the city. Dad was appreciating your short speech,' she said, with a tinge of laughter.

'I only did what was necessary,' I replied with a tone of indifference.

'Dad was saying there is a politician in you. You are charismatic, composed and empathetic. Just like your father,' she said, proudly.

'Really?' I scoffed.

'It was hard,' I said after a moment.

'I can understand,' she said softly. 'Should I catch the tomorrow morning flight?'

'No no, please. I'll come back in a few days anyway. Give me some time. Let things settle down here and then I'll come back,' I assured her.

We changed the topic of our conversation and discussed about her campus placement interview. She told me she had a job offer from Amazon. They were willing to offer her twenty-two lakhs to take up a position in their Delhi office.

'It's perfect, Boo! Why do you sound upset?' I was puzzled.

'Because you're not here. They want me to sign the contract for one year. What if you don't crack a job in Delhi? What if you are placed somewhere in Hyderabad or some other place? What will I do here alone?' she answered.

'Don't miss this opportunity, Boo! I'll be there with you. You can't leave this perfect job with the perfect package. And what if I don't make it in Delhi? I'll choose that job which can keep me in Delhi,' I replied.

'And package?' she asked.

'That's not important as long as we are together, isn't it? I wish to spend the rest of my life with you. This is what I want,' I added.

'Thank you so much, for being so supportive, Dravya. I will sign the contract then,' she said after a moment.

'Not at all, Shagun. You are a very dedicated person; you had worked so hard for your dreams. Nothing should stop you from taking flight. The sky is the limit,' I said.

Shagun took a sigh of relief and smiled. She was eternally grateful to that moment when her beautiful journey with Dravya started. And the rest, as they say, is history.

The Settlement

'Is it okay now?' I adjusted the pillows and made my dad lay down on his bed. We were at home.

'Yes, now it's fine,' he said, making himself comfortable.

'The doctor and the two nurses will be here twenty-four hours for you. I've told them to be here for a week,' I looked at them and said.

'They don't need to be here, Dravya. I'm completely alright now,' he said.

'That's what we said to your son in the hospital, Sethji. But your son, he brought us here,' the doctor said.

'Why, Dravya?' He turned to me.

'Because I think it's necessary, Dad. It's just a matter of a week. What if you relapse? I don't want to take any risk,' I responded.

'But there is no risk anymore. I just have to be on medication, right?' He turned to the doctor.

'Yes sir!' The doctor replied.

'Can you give us five minutes?' He looked at everyone and said.

'Come, sit near me!' He gestured to me. Everyone left the room and I sat next to my dad.

'I heard you gave a short syrupy speech the day I was shot and admitted?'

I nodded.

'Don't you want to know who told me?' he asked.

'Mom must have,' I guessed.

'Anand Bhushan,' he said.

'Anand Bhushan, that VPJ politician?' I spoke in amazement.

'Yes! They want to make an alliance,' Dad said after a pause.

'For the upcoming Rajya Sabha election?' My eyes grew wide.

'Yes, they think we can work together and form a government. We have a very strong chance of forming the government with them if we give them 600 crore rupees.'

'And what do we get?' I asked.

'I become the Home Minister,' he replied.

'What?' My eyes grew in amazement. 'Really?'

'They have assured me. We'll take advantage of my attack and get votes. This time, the entire Varanasi is with us. What do you think?'

'That's great, Dad. We should surely go for an alliance then,' I opined.

'But Dravya, you'll have to stay here with me. Look after our business and help me in the election. You can't expect me to juggle everything,' he said.

'And my degree?'

'That's not a knotty problem. Election is in seven months and your final semester will end soon. You can have your degree, but please, no job. Why do you want to work for someone else when you can earn in crores here? Beta, I have toiled all my life to earn what we have today. Now it's time to take a leap and do something big. We have had enough of MLA posts,' he said.

'I was thinking of joining your business in two years,' I said in my defense.

'You've to take responsibility now, Dravya. You can't ruin this opportunity. We'll never have this opportunity back,' he added.

'You're right, Dad,' I said pondering. 'Home Ministry is not a matter of joke. Hmm, let's do this!' I kept my hand on his and said smiling.

'Home Minister, huh?' I smiled.

'See, I told you. This is why I didn't want to sign the contract.' We were on a video call. 'Now I'm stuck in Delhi for a year. What will I do here alone?' she said.

'What can I do, Boo? Even this is important.'

'I knew things would change and that's why I didn't want to take any chance. I didn't want to join Amazon, but you forced me to, and made me sign the contract.'

'Boo?' I said softly.

'What?' she responded after a while.

'You have to understand,' I insisted.

'I trusted you, Boo,' her tone changed.

'I understand, but...'

'But I don't understand what I'm supposed to do now,' she crossed me.

'I'm sorry,' I said in a low tone.

'What will your sorry do?'

'Then what do you want me to do? You want me to leave my dad and stay with you?'

'I didn't say that,' she said quickly.

'You don't want my dad to become Home Minister?' I asked.

'Boo, I never said that,' she repeated.

'Then what do you want?' I said louder.

'I just want to live with you,' she said softly.

Her calm voice silenced me. The louder I spoke, the softer her voice became. I took a moment and then said, 'Boo, this is what you wanted, right? You wanted to have a successful career as a corporate professional. I just wanted a degree for the sake of it. You can work for a year and then come back to Varanasi if you want.'

'If I want? Of course I'm going to do that now. You want me to stay here for long?' She sounded irritated.

'No, I don't want that,' I replied. 'I want you to be by my side.'

'I am! I am always by your side. And I'm sorry, I think I overreacted. Your family is important too. I want uncle to win this election.' Her voice reflected her smile.

'Thank you for understanding, Boo. And one year is nothing, it will just pass by,' I comforted her.

So this was the settlement made. I'd return after final semester exams and help my dad in his election campaign and business. Shagun would return after a year.

It was my fault. I had forced her to sign the contract. I wish I hadn't done that. And honestly speaking, I wouldn't have let her sign the contract if I knew about the alliance and my dad's decision earlier.

We both could return after the exams together. And once again, it was she who was ready to compromise for our relationship. She was ready to quit the MNC job after three years of experience and she was ready to quit even now. All she wanted was to be with me forever. We were meant to be together.

'Are you sure?' My anger burst out.

'Yes,' Vijay said. 'DSP confirmed.'

'Did you tell dad about it?'

'No, not yet. I thought of telling you first,' he said.

'And who else knows?' I asked.

'Malik,' he replied.

'Tell Malik not to share this with dad,' I ordered.

'But why? He should know. Sethji will handle it himself.'

'No, Vijay. He just recovered. I don't want any stress for him.'

DSP Singh called up Vijay and told him about the mastermind behind my dad's attack. It was Mukesh Tripathi, who was expecting a seat in the upcoming elections. My dad was a token to the seat and he was my dad's fierce competitor. A spy informed the DSP about the sniper who had been arrested, but informally.

'Call the DSP and fix a meeting with Mukesh Tripathi,' I said.

'Wait here, you can't go in,' one of the guards in a safari suit with thick moustache stopped us outside Tripathi's office.

'Please don't do that,' a man in mid-fifties, wearing a white crisp kurta pajama walked out and said looking at me.

'They are our important guests today,' he joined his palms and said.

'Who is he?' I bent towards Malik and whispered.

'Mukesh Tripathi,' he replied softly.

'Please, come in,' Tripathi walked in and we followed. 'Coffee or juice?' he asked after we settled down.

'Nothing, thank you,' I said.

'You've come to my office for the first time, I won't let you go this way.' He kept smiling. I couldn't believe his unimpeachable smile.

'Jitu, orange juice, quick!' he said to a guy standing near the gate.

'So, how's Sethji?' Tripathi sipped his juice and asked. 'Is he doing well now?'

'You're worried about him?' I asked.

'Yes, of course. After all, he's our MLA,' he said showing fake concern.

'You should try your luck in movies, sometimes. You will play a good villain, like Amrish Puri.' I gave a sarcastic laugh.

'What do you mean?' His brows furrowed.

'You know well what I'm talking about,' I said.

'Don't tell me you doubt my intentions. I am a social worker who strives to serve my people. Killing people is not my profession,' he said.

'One, I didn't say anything about killing anyone. And two, the police arrested a sniper yesterday,' I said.

'Really?' Tripathi took out his cell phone and started working on it. 'Did he say something?'

I didn't say a word. I kept gazing at him.

Tripathi looked at me and said, 'Now don't tell me he took my name.'

'You tell me, did he?' I asked a rhetorical question.

'The elections are here, Dravya. It is all blame game. And mud-slinging is a part of the process,' Tripathi defended himself.

'And now you can go and ask the sniper again. I'm sure he won't take my name this time.' He pressed the lock button of his cell phone and said.

'Don't believe these idiots, Dravya. Sethji is smart. He knows the tricks of the trade.'

'Call him Baba,' Malik interrupted.

'He's baba for you folks, not for me,' Tripathi lit his cigar and said.

'Right, Dravya?' He turned to me.

'Yes,' I bit my lower lips and said.

'So what can I do for you?' He filled the environment with menacing smoke.

'Nothing, I just came to see you. I came to wish you luck for the upcoming elections, ' I replied.

'That's it?' He voiced, startled.

'Yes.' I stood up.

'And your juice? You didn't even touch the glass,' he asked.

'We'll meet soon.' I smiled.

'Sure!' He walked till the door with us.

'Keep your promise. You said we'll meet soon,' he said, joining his hands.

I still couldn't believe his audacity and cocky smile.

'Don't worry, we are meeting soon.'

'And take care of Sethji. People are ready to take lives for a very small amount these days. Today's youth, I tell you,' he kept his hand on my shoulder and said.

I shrugged and said, 'I can take care of my dad.'

'That's good. Let us just hope for the best.' He nodded.

My anger was fuming inside. I was so furious that I wanted to kill Tripathi right at that very moment. He threatened my dad and I couldn't do anything. I was shocked at his courage to scare us. It required a lot of guts to threaten the Seth family. I resolved to teach him a lesson.

'He's very smart,' I said after sitting in the car.

'You didn't talk much. I wonder why we came here,' Malik sounded puzzled.

'I came here to see the face of that man who tried to get my dad killed. He is a dangerous man. After all, he is such an important political player.'

'He is! Don't go on his innocent smile,' Malik added.

'Increase dad's security. The way he kept his hand on my shoulder, I think he's planning for something. No one should be allowed around dad. His security is our top priority,' I commanded.

I wouldn't have thought twice before getting the bugger killed, but elections were near and I didn't want to take a risk before that. He had threatened me about my dad, but nothing could be done right now. We had to win this election first. For now, we had to stay quiet. We couldn't put at stake the sympathy wave in our favour right now.

'What do we do?' Malik asked.

'Focus on dad's security and well-being. We will wait for the right moment to take revenge from him. After winning the election, we will kill Tripathi,' I turned to him and said.

'Should we tell Sethji about today's meeting? And about the sniper?' he asked next.

'No no, let us keep this between both of us. We should not escalate it. Let's leave him. We can deal with everything after the election.'

'What?' I stood aghast. 'When?'

'Just now,' Malik replied.

'But how can this happen?' I was still in shock.

'It happened, Baba. DSP confirmed.'

'Who can do this?' Malik wondered.

'Mukesh Tripathi?' I mumbled.

'Yes!' he confirmed.

Malik had just got information about the sniper, who was now lying dead in jail. Few men had been arrested and kept in the same cell as the sniper. They murdered him. The sniper was arrested without the formal paperwork, so there was nothing on record. The DSP was waiting for our order to file the chargesheet.

I'd told him to wait until my meeting with Tripathi and then I would decide what to do next. Malik called up the DSP to release the sniper and he got the information about what happened.

'Dispose the body and don't let anyone know,' I said.

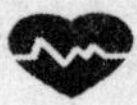

'Can I come to the airport tomorrow?' Shagun asked me in her perky tone.

I was appalled and at a loss for words. It was hard to believe how Tripathi could do all that in such a short time span. His roots were stout. I was lost in my thoughts when Shagun's voice got me out of it.

'Boo?' I heard Shagun calling me on phone.

'Yes!' I responded.

'Should I come to the airport tomorrow?' she asked.

'No,' I said softly.

'But why...?' She pulled her last word. 'I want to come.'

I remained quiet.

'I don't think I'm catching my flight tomorrow,' I said.

'What?' She reacted.

'But why?' she asked.

'I have to stay with my dad here,' I answered.

'What happened to uncle? Is he alright?' She asked with genuine concern in her voice.

I told Shagun about the meeting with Tripathi and what he said when we were leaving his office. I even told her what happened in the police station.

'So you think uncle can be attacked again?'

I answered in affirmation.

'But why didn't you let the DSP file the chargesheet when the sniper had admitted that Tripathi was behind all this?' Shagun asked.

'I thought this would bring Tripathi in the limelight and at this stage, we couldn't think of doing this mistake. We could do the settlement after election.'

'Some of the policemen can also be on his side. I mean, those men who were arrested today were kept in the same cell; that can't be a coincidence,' Shagun said.

'That's what Vijay was saying. But we deal with all this after elections. For now, I have to be here to protect my dad. Even if I have to quit my Master's, I will do it. My family is most important to me.'

'I agree. Protecting uncle should be our first priority,' Shagun said quickly. 'You should stay there,' she added.

'Thank you for understanding, Boo,' I said in a loving tone.

Two Hundred Crores

So, this is how my political career started.

The party flags and hoardings were installed everywhere in the city, as well as the rest of the state. I realized my strength and contribution in the election after I saw my photo beside my dad in every hoarding.

'So finally politics, huh?' Sid said. We were talking on phone.

'I don't know, Sid. I really don't know when and how all this happened. I was only here to fortify dad,' I added.

'And now you're on every hoarding. I knew this would happen. Simmi and I were sure this would happen one day. But you always ignored the fact. I heard uncle is going to Delhi to raise funds for election?' Sid asked.

'Yes, he went two days back. He's returning today. He must have landed by now,' I said looking at the wall clock.

'By the way, who's in Delhi?' Sid asked.

'I don't know, some old friends. Have you heard of Dreambricks in Delhi? Suraj Mahajan is the MD of the company. You know, big election, big fund. You need rich people for that. So dad will leverage his old connection to raise funds. He's expecting two hundred crores from Dreambricks,' I answered.

'Wow! That's a whopping amount. Will they give it?' Sid asked.

'They should, or else dad would never fly to Delhi. Dad will persuade them to expand in UP after the elections. Something like you help me, I help you...'

'Yeah, I got you. Together we grow sort of thing,' Sid said.

'Anyway, how's your job going?' I asked to change the topic.

'It sucks man! I really want to go back to college.'

'Why, what happened?' I guffawed.

'You won't understand. Once you start working for someone else, you will realize. All the time, yes sir, no sir, ok sir... What's all this, man?'

'You can come back here too.' I laughed.

'Oh please, and do what there? I don't want to be a part of my ancestral business. I can't do that,' he answered.

'Then keep doing yes sir, no sir, ok sir.' I burst out laughing.

I was still talking to Sid when the notification of my phone indicated a WhatsApp message. I checked and saw that it was dad's message. He had sent me a photo of a girl. I ignored and kept talking to Sid. My phone beeped again, dad's call was waiting.

'Sid, I'll talk to you later. Dad is on call waiting,' I declined his call and received the other call. 'Yes Dad!'

'Dravya?' I heard his voice.

'Did you see the photo?' he asked.

'Yes, yes, I saw the photo,' I said.

'Did you like her, Dravya?' He asked excitedly.

'Like her, as in?' I wondered.

'You know what I mean, Dravya. I'm talking about your marriage.'

'My marriage?' I sounded terrified. 'Where did this come from?'

'Real estate Dreambricks is funding us in this election. He's my good friend, Dravya. They want to take this friendship to the next level. They have proposed to solidify our relationship by offering us cash and their daughter together.'

'But how can this happen?' I was shocked. 'I mean...'

'Where are you right now?' he asked.

'I'm at home,' I replied. 'Let us talk on this after dinner.'

Suraj Mahajan of Dreambricks had heard my speech on the day my dad was shot. Since then, he was convinced that I was born to be an influential politician. My dad's happiness knew no bounds when he received the proposal. He was just asking me as a formality. Even my mom happily agreed after seeing Khushi's photo. According to her, she had never seen as beautiful a girl as Khushi. I wondered what would be her reaction if I brought Shagun in front of her. Would she believe her eyes?

Dreambricks was ready to help us with two hundred crores. They were ready to have the engagement before the elections and the marriage would take place after the elections.

'I don't think I'm ready for this marriage,' I said.

'What?' Dad looked at me. He then turned to mom.

'But why?' Mom asked me.

'I don't like the girl,' I said after a pause.

'You don't like the girl?' Dad was startled. 'What do you mean by you don't like the girl?'

'Dravya, look at me,' Mom said softly.

'Khushi is a pretty girl. She's from a reputed wealthy family. She is doing her Bachelor's in Economics from St. Stephen's college. What else do you look for in a girl?'

'I don't know, but...'

'But what?' Dad said quickly.

'But I don't like the girl,' I said looking into his eyes.

'Have you gone crazy, Dravya? What's wrong with you? Two hundred crores is not a joke,' He unleashed his fury on me.

'I didn't say that,' I responded.

'Then, give us one good reason to reject this girl,' he asked, anger dripping from his voice.

'I don't have any solid reason, but I don't think I'm ready,' I mustered some courage to answer back.

'Your son is going crazy with every day,' he turned to Mom.

'Two hundred crores beta, two hundred crores! This huge amount can help us in winning the elections. Think about your party, your dad...' Her voice shook.

'I'm still not ready, Mom,' I said and stood up to leave.

'Dravya, at this point, we neither have the time nor the energy to waste on these pointless discussions,' Dad said. 'You agree or we give up this election.'

I didn't say a word. I walked off to my room quickly.

'Dravya,' he called me. I did not respond.

'Dravya,' he yelled.

'Dravya...'

The Exit Plan

The tranquillity of my life had been disrupted. Everything was falling apart. My dad's proposal had ripped off all the happiness from my life. It brought me to a very difficult crossroad.

What should I choose? My love for Shagun or my duty as a son for my family?

I was sad beyond measure. I was seeking for a ray of light which could get me out of this dark tunnel.

Khushi's family came to Varanasi to meet my family. A formal meeting was fixed for both of us so that we could know each other. I did not wish to know about her. I was doing all this to raise funds. That's it!

'You don't want to ask me anything?' Khushi said to break the silence.

'No,' I kept stirring the straw of my drink. 'You?' I looked up to her.

She was beautiful, but nothing compared to my Shagun. She was fair, thin and tall, maybe three inches below me. Her eyes, they were not like Shagun's. They were a little smaller. I did not feel connected when I looked into her eyes. She had a pleasant smile but it exuded the warmth of a sincere friend. Her cherry colour suit with golden work suited her well.

'I asked what I had to,' she replied.

'So, shall we leave?' I sounded restless.

'You're sure you don't want to ask anything?' she said.

'Our parents are ready, what can I say?' I said reluctantly.

'Yeah, still...' she insisted.

'No, nothing.' I gave a fake smile.

'I thought you would ask me so many questions.' She smiled.

'Hmm...' I nodded. Her dad was funding us two hundred crores. Did I need anything else!

Khushi wanted us to get engaged, but she was not ready for marriage right now. She was in her final year and wanted to do her Master's in Economics before getting married. And this was my blind spot. I had a perfect scheme to evade the chaos now.

'Thank you for understanding, Dravya,' she said.

'Thank you for giving me my blind spot,' I said to myself.

It was all set. Before Khushi left, she asked me for my cell phone number, which I had to give her. I just couldn't take two hundred crores and say I don't want to talk to you.

'Is it true?' Simmi asked me as soon as I received her call.

'You're getting engaged?' Her voice rose.

'Yes,' I said softly.

'And what about Shagun?' she wondered.

'We have to win this election at any cost,' I took a moment to reply.

'What about Shagun, Dravya? I thought you loved her.' She got restless.

'I still love her,' I answered.

'No, you don't! If you really loved her, then you would never do this,' she said.

'I'm doing this for my dad. I am helpless, Simmi.'

'Leaving Shagun forever for your dad? Tell me, how much did you sell yourself for? I heard it's 200 crores. How could you do this, Dravya?' Her tone turned soft. 'Have you thought of Shagun?'

'I'm still thinking of her,' I said.

'Then don't do this. What you're going to do will turn out to be the biggest mistake of your life. You'll never be able to reverse things. There is no going back from here.'

'How do we win this election then? No matter how much popular support we have, funding is always the game-changer. And, for becoming the Home Minister, we need enormous funds,' I defended myself.

'To hell with your election and your Home Minister, Dravya. What's wrong with you?' She roared with rage. 'Just don't do this!'

'Everything is set now. I can't step back,' I said.

'Then congratulations for this huge mistake. And let me tell you, it's a wrong decision,' she said and disconnected the call.

'And by the way, have you spoken to Shagun about this?' She asked straight when she called me for the second time.

'No,' I replied.

'Very good! When is the engagement?'

'Next week, Christmas. We are having the engagement in Delhi. At Lodhi from 6 PM onwards,' I replied.

'Great, Dravya, great!' she said sarcastically and handed over the phone to Sid.

'Hello, what are you up to, bro? Why are you doing this?' I heard Sid's voice.

'Listen to me, Sid. Listen to me first. Even though I am getting engaged with this girl, I will not marry her. As per her conditions, she wants to complete her Master's in Economics first and then get married.'

'How do you know?' He asked.

'I met her,' I took a deep breath and said.

'What? You even met her? When? Where?' Sid sounded perplexed.

'A few days back,' I replied.

'What's happening, Dravya? You've messed up everything all of a sudden.' He sounded worried.

'At this point of time, Sid, all I can say is we need enormous funding to win this election, which only Dreambricks can give us. We don't have time and we don't have anyone else left who can fund us.'

'So as per your plan, you get engaged, raise funds, win the elections, and then break this relationship before that girl completes her Master's?' He shared his conjecture.

'Yes! And I'll make sure Dreambricks earns 200 crores through me before I call off this marriage,' I completed his sentence.

'This is wrong, Dravya. What you're doing is wrong. You are ruining two lives here, for both Shagun and Khushi.'

'I'm helpless, Sid. Everything is at stake here. We've already raised funds to win this election, and if we lose, we lose everything. And I can't let that happen,' I responded with conviction in my voice.

'And Shagun?' Sid asked after a pause. 'Will she agree?'

'She has to,' I replied.

'What if she doesn't?'

'Then I don't know,' I said. 'She has to have faith in me,' I added.

'Will she agree? I mean, we all know her very well. Her vision, her expectations from you and her life...'

'I'll take care of everything,' I said again.

'You can't do this, Boo. Please don't do this,' her voice broke as she said those words. We were talking over phone and I had told Shagun everything.

'You can't leave me in the middle of nowhere. I am coming to meet you,' she said. 'We can meet and talk, and sort out things.'

'I'm coming to Delhi next week,' I said.

'But you're coming for your engagement. And you can't do this. What about us?' she was apprehensive.

'I've told you, Boo. I'm doing this engagement only to raise funds. I'm not going to marry her. I love you, only you,' I tried to comfort her.

'Please Boo, please don't do this. I'm begging you. You vowed to live your life only with me.' I heard her crying on the phone.

'And I'll keep that promise,' I said.

'You don't have to do this.' She could barely speak.

'I'm not getting married, Boo. It's just the engagement. We have spent five years together. Have faith in me. I'll handle everything.'

'I don't wanna lose you, Boo. I don't even wanna imagine doing that. Please, you don't have to do this.' She pleaded.

'Do you trust me?' I asked after a moment.

'Yes, yes, I trust you,' she said quickly.

'Then stay with me, nothing will happen.'

'I'm coming tomorrow to meet you,' she said after a pause.

'Are you crazy? No, please, you don't have to,' I said a little louder. 'There is no point coming here.'

'I'm coming,' she said confidently.

'Boo, please!'

'I'm coming. I'm coming to stop you. You do your job and I will do mine,' she said and hung up the phone.

Take your Pick

Love is crazy, isn't it? The path of true love is always riddled with obstacles.

But you believe you can win any battle. Even when things are not in your favour, you have the unflinching support from your partner, which does not let you crumble. I was expecting the same kind of faith from Shagun. Even though life took us on a different path, I believed that, by the end, everything will work in our favour. I wish I was right.

'Where are you?' Shagun asked me after I received her call.

'I'm in a meeting,' I covered my lips and whispered as softly as I could. 'Why, what happened?'

'I've landed,' she said.

'What?' My whisper rose. 'You're in Varanasi?'

'Yes,' she replied.

'What are you doing here? I mean, why?' I pulled my last word.

'You know why I'm here. We need to talk,' she said.

'Excuse me,' I looked around at the people in the meeting and walked out.

'Why, Boo?' My voice turned normal.

'I told you I was coming to Delhi next week,' I said firmly.

I took a deep breath and said, 'Fine, go home, let me finish my work and then we can meet in the evening.'

'I'm not going home,' she said.

'What? What do you mean by you're not going home?' I sounded perplexed. 'Where will you go then?'

'I'll wait for you,' she replied.

'I'm in middle of my meeting. It will take me time. Please go home,' I requested her.

'I'm ready to meet you in the evening, but I'm not going home,' she said. Her voice said how confident she was.

'Then what will you do here?' I asked.

'The city belongs to me as much as it belongs to you. You don't have to worry about me here. Just finish everything and meet me,' she said.

'And what will you do till then?' I asked.

'I'm going to Dashashwamedh Ghat where you promised me that we'll live together forever. You can come there when you're done with all your work,' she said.

'Boo, please, don't mess up anything right now. I'm already under a lot of pressure, I can't deal with this anymore.'

'I'm waiting at the ghat,' she said after a pause, and disconnected the call.

I walked in to continue the meeting, but I could barely sit there for five minutes. Shagun was in town and I couldn't resist myself. Every part of my body wanted to meet her, hold her and embrace her. My eyes turned desperate as they wanted to catch a glimpse of her. I kept bouncing my right leg on my toe, probably I was nervous. I was no longer focused in the meeting.

I wanted to walk out. I wanted to meet Shagun. When I couldn't hold it any longer, I stood up.

'I'm sorry,' I said and stopped bouncing my leg. 'I have to leave.'

I glanced through the file and said, 'We meet tomorrow at the same time and continue from here. Will that work?'

The four men looked at each other, startled, and one of them said, 'Sure.'

'Fine,' I walked out of the meeting.

My car halted at the end of the lane where vehicles were not permitted to be parked. I got down from the car and rushed towards the ghat. My eyes searched for her.

'Shagun,' I screamed and strode downstairs close to Ganga where Shagun was sitting.

Shagun turned back and stood up screaming, 'Boo...'

We finally met after months and hugged each other. We embraced, a tight clasp with cheeks brushing past each other. I was missing her aroma which I finally had back. Her arms were where I belonged. It was the safest place in the world. It seemed as if time froze for both of us. We wanted to live the moment to the fullest...

'Boo?' she whispered.

'Shh...'

I was still not ready to talk. In that embrace, I felt that all the broken pieces of my life were coming together. Our connection was divine.

'Boo,' she slowly pushed me away.

It was then when I looked at her properly. Her hair, her clothes, everything was in disarray.

'What have you done to yourself?' I gazed at her from top to bottom. 'You came here like this?'

'Boo, please don't do this,' she was too choked with emotions to speak.

Her clothes were shabby, as if she didn't bother about what she was wearing when she took off from Delhi. Dishevelled hair, eyes swollen up, as if she hadn't slept all night. The eyeliner was partially rubbed off. It seemed that she had been crying for long hours. Her nose was a little red and her lustrous skin looked faded.

'You came all the way from Delhi, this way?' I looked at her flip-flops and asked. I was feeling bad for her.

'What have you made yourself?' I touched her smudged eyeliner mark, dried up with tears.

'Just don't do this,' she said, sobbing. 'I won't let you do this.'

'Boo,' I took her face in my palms and wiped away her tears with both my thumbs.

'Have you looked at yourself? Why all this?' I asked softly.

'I don't care about my looks. I don't care about anything. Just don't do this, please.' Her tears rolled down again.

'Come, let's sit somewhere and talk. Have you eaten anything?'

'Yes,' she nodded.

'Yes? Really? Swear on me?'

She buried her face and shook her head in a no.

'No? Why?'

She didn't reply.

'Boo…' My eyes grew with voice. 'Why?' I turned soft and hugged her.

Shagun clasped my shirt's collar from behind and collapsed in my arms, crying. I had never seen Shagun like this. I could feel how broken she was in my arms. My tears rolled down too.

'Boo, please, please don't leave me,' her voice slurred. 'I want to die in your arms. I think I have made some grave mistake. The winds of change are frightening me. Destiny is not in my favour.' She choked.

'Time and destiny are with us. You just have to stay strong and be by my side,' I said soothing her.

'No, Boo. I don't know why, but I don't feel very optimistic.'

'Shh… Stay quiet and relax,' I said, soothing her. Once she had gained some composure, I asked, 'You want to go home?'

'No,' she replied.

'Why? Do your parents know that you are in Varanasi?'

Shagun shook her head in the negative. I was surprised. Shagun was a very mature and responsible girl. She was known for handling stressful situations really well. But, this seemed to be a very erratic step from her.

'I came to stop you,' she said looking into my eyes. 'You can't ditch me.'

'I'm not ditching you. I can never do that,' I responded.

'Then call off this engagement.' She raised her voice.

'It's just a compromise. You have to understand this. Come, I will explain everything to you. Let's go to the hotel first. Where is your bag?' I looked around.

'I didn't bring any bag,' she said.

'What? You just came?' I was startled.

'Let's go to the hotel first,' I said in a soft tone. 'We shouldn't create a scene here, Boo. We have elections in February,' I clutched her hand and pulled her to my car.

'Anything else, Baba?' The manager asked after unlocking the door.

'Nothing, thank you.' He left and we entered the room. 'Mishra ji?' I gave a call.

The manager turned back and scurried towards me.

'Get me something to eat, something quick.'

'Sure Baba.' He nodded and left.

'Do you want to hit the shower? Should I arrange for some clothes for you?' I asked after locking the door from inside.

'Just call off this engagement,' she said.

I took a deep breath and said, 'The food is arriving. You should freshen up.'

'I'm not here to eat. I'm not here to have a shower. Just give me what I want and then I'll do whatever you say.' She shouted in anger.

'Boo…' I went close to her. 'Listen to me…'

'No, you listen to me,' she interrupted me in the middle and said, 'What do you want from me? How can I stop you?' Her tears rolled down while speaking. She slumped on the bed and sat covering her face. I sat beside her.

'I'll die without you, Boo,' she looked up and said.

'Can't you stop this?' she choked.

'It's not possible,' I said and my tears rolled down after seeing Shagun's eyes wet.

'You know what's happening is wrong. You know everything very well, right? You were here to protect your dad, not to get trapped into these dirty political games and gimmicks. We're supposed to be together.'

'But Boo…'

'No. Just do as I'm saying. Call off this engagement!' she ordered me.

'What do you want from me? You want me to look into your eyes and say I love you? I can do that.'

'I love you, I love you,' she pulled me closer.

'See, I can do that. I'm not shy anymore. I love you,' she said once again and pecked me on my lips. 'See, I can do that too,' she pecked once again and said quickly. 'I can be the first one to kiss you,' she kept kissing all over my face.

Her words gusted out in a wave of uninhibited emotion. They pierced my soul.

'You want to make love?' She unzipped her jacket.

'I'm not shy anymore. You can do whatever you want.'

'Boo,' I caught her hand. I slowly zipped up her jacket.

'Please don't do this with me,' she said.

'I'm in love with who you are, not with what you can turn into. You don't have to do this. 'I'm in love with you, I love you.' I hugged her.

Shagun clasped me in her arms and said, 'I love you too. I love you too.' She started sobbing.

She was completely broken.

Someone knocked at the door.

'Boo, food arrived,' I said.

'I don't want to eat,' she said remaining in the same position.

'But why? You must be hungry.'

'I'm not hungry,' she said softly.

'I know why you're saying this. You want to make me eat.'

'No, I'm really hungry,' I smiled.

'Really?' She left me and asked looking at me.

'Yes,' I nodded.

"I wiped her tears and she wiped mine."

'Take some more rice,' I offered her.

'No, I'm done,' she caught my hand to stop me. 'This is my last spoon,' she lifted hers and said.

'Call off your engagement,' she kept the spoon in her plate.

'Boo, I told you. It's just a compromise. I'm not getting married to her. Give me some time, I'll break this engagement.' I tried to convince her.

'By ruining that girl's life? You can't do this to her. This will not make anyone happy.'

'How do we win elections then? How will my dad get Home Minister's post?'

'Your dad can remain the MLA here. Be happy with that. You can't ravage so many lives for a chair. Our relationship matters to you, right?' she asked.

'It does,' I replied.

'Then don't do this. Don't be a politician and manipulate others for your own vested interests,' she said.

'And what if I tell you I can't do that?'

'Call off this engagement or else...'

'Or else...?'

'You take your call. I can't be a part of this scam.' She paused for a moment to utter these words.

'You know what? I thought if I come to Varanasi, I'll be able to stop you. But it seems you have made up your mind. There is no going back for you,' she said.

'We have to win this election, that's all I know.'

'So you're still ready for this engagement?' she confirmed.

'I have to do this,' I said.

'Don't do this. I can't handle this. I'm begging you, please,' she clasped my hand and her voice broke, sobbing. 'You'll lose everything one day.'

'I can't help it,' I said.

'Fine,' she left my hand and wiped her tears.

'Take care,' her tears fell which she wiped and took a step when I caught her hand and asked, 'Where are you going?'

'You shouldn't be bothered,' she released her hand and walked to the gate.

'Boo,' I stood up and followed her.

'You've changed a lot, Boo. It's over for me now. You have immersed yourself so much in elections that you're not seeing what you're losing. Take care,' she said and walked off.

I didn't stop her. Even though I let her go, I was crushed. Where would Shagun go? She was mine, after all. I believed in the power of our love. Even though the times are difficult, I had immense faith in our relationship. We had diligently worked hard to strengthen our bond over these years. I was certain that we would pass the test of time and emerge victorious.

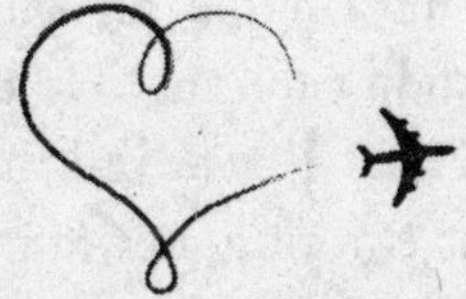

The Agony of Separation

'What? How can she do this?' I was dumbstruck.

'You got engaged to Khushi. What do you expect from her?' Simmi said.

'This can't be happening,' I muttered in shock. 'When is she leaving?' I asked.

'Tomorrow, evening flight,' Simmi replied on phone.

'And you're telling me now?' I replied in anger.

'Don't shout at me, Dravya. You're responsible for all this. She flew to Varanasi to stop you. Even after returning to Delhi, she kept begging you over phone. How much do you expect from people to beg in front of you? Eventually, they will move on,' Simmi's voice rose.

Amazon offered Shagun an onsite opportunity to join their office in the London branch, which she accepted. They were transferring her, extending the agreement for the next four years.

'Stop her,' I said softly. 'Do something, don't let her go.'

'She won't stop now, Dravya. I've already spoken to her.'

'What did she say?' My voice turned anxious.

'She's done with you!' Simmi said after a pause.

Simmi wanted to inform me all this earlier, but Shagun stopped her. Even Sid didn't tell me. He didn't want to meddle anymore. He even said that I deserved this. He said that I had ruined Shagun's life, her emotion, her faith, everything.

'But I did all this to win this election,' I defended myself.

'You know what, Dravya? I still do not believe that you are not willing to see your mistakes. You are so self-absorbed. Why don't you accept that what you have done is very selfish? What's wrong with you? You're so engrossed in expanding your power that you don't know what you're losing.'

'The election starts from next week,' I brooded over and said.

'Still... election? Really? Fuck off, Dravya Seth!' She hung up on me.

'Dravya? What are you doing here?' Shagun was perturbed as soon as she opened the door.

'You won't ask me to come in?' I said.

'I don't have much time. And, I don't think we have anything to talk about anymore.'

'Not even five minutes for me? For your Boo?'

'Okay!' she thought for a while and let me in.

'Please, have a seat,' she offered me.

'Why so formal, Boo?' I said after sitting down. I sat on a sofa and Shagun sat on a bean bag which was placed at some distance.

'Why are you here?' she asked.

'To stop you,' I replied.

'To stop me? Do you think you can?' she tried to challenge me.

'Yes!' I asserted.

'I don't think so. You're wrong, once again,' she said.

'Why are you doing this? Why are you running away?' I asked.

'I'm not running away. You did what you had to and now I'm doing what I think is correct for me,' she said.

'This is right for you? For us?' I asked.

'There is no "us" here, not anymore,' she said, trying to control her emotions.

'So you have made up your mind?'

'Yes.' Her tears rolled down.

'I'm begging you,' my tears were on edge.

'Even I was begging you that day. Did you listen to me?' she questioned me.

'Did you listen to me, Dravya?' Her voice rose. 'How could you do that? You got engaged to that girl and I'm sure you must have got funded, as promised. You're winning this election, congratulations to you and to your dad. You got everything you wanted.' She smiled feebly.

'Boo,' I crawled on my knees to her. 'Don't do this, please,' I begged. 'I'm begging you, don't go anywhere,' I clasped her hand.

'Don't touch me,' she released her hand and pushed me away in wrath. I fell on the floor. I let my whole body go limp.

'Boo,' she instantly responded and came to lift me. 'You okay? I'm sorry.'

'Please don't go anywhere. You can't leave me,' I said, sobbing.

'I have to, I've signed the contract.'

'You didn't ask me before signing,' my voice broke.

'Even you didn't ask me before exchanging the rings. You took your call and I took mine.'

'Boo, don't go anywhere, give me some time.' I hugged her, crying. 'Don't give me two years. Just give me this year. Just give me this year and we can be together, like always. I'll cancel my wedding by end of this year.'

'What you did with me was wrong, Boo. Don't do the same with Khushi. You have no right to besmirch someone's reputation and life,' she said with a tone of compassion.

'But Boo...'

'Shh...' She soothed me. 'No matter how much you try now, you can never bring us together.'

'But...' I tried to speak.

'You can't stop me, like I couldn't stop you,' she said.

'Boo...'

'You did what you had to.'

'Boo, let me speak. Let me complete my sentence,' I screamed.

'I know what you want to say. I'm sorry but I can't stay. I have to leave.'

'Then go, just go away!' I yelled and pushed her in fury.

Shagun stumbled, but it was so quick that she couldn't keep her balance. The push was so hard and sudden that she hit her head on the corner of the table.

'Boo,' I reacted and gripped her in my arms.

She pressed her forehead through which blood trickled. I was completely blank after seeing her blood. I was so numb, I didn't know what I was supposed to do.

'I'm sorry,' I said quickly and removed her hand from her forehead to see her wound.

She covered her forehead again and stood up stumbling. I once again gripped her in my arms.

'Let me go,' she tried to release herself from me.

'Listen, Boo...'

Before I could say a word more, she pushed me away. 'Thank you for everything. I think you should leave now,' she said.

'Your wound...'

'It's okay now, you don't have to worry,' she said quickly. 'I can take care of myself.'

She went to the bathroom and locked herself inside.

'Boo,' I banged the door.

'Boo,' I banged again.

'Open the door, open the door, Boo.' I kept knocking. 'Are you okay?'

I was distraught. I know whatever happened shouldn't have happened and I hadn't done purposely. It was just an accident. But when things are not in your favour, every well-intended action turns out to be a mishappening.

Shagun finally unlocked the door and walked out of the bathroom.

'You okay?' I asked looking at the band-aid on her forehead.

'Yes,' she nodded with tears in her eyes.

'I am sorry,' I took a step closer.

'I don't have time for all this. I'm getting late. Simmi and Sid are waiting for me at the airport,' her voice quivered.

She collected a few more things quickly and zipped her bag.

'Got to go,' she stood in front of me.

'Boo,' I mumbled, tears rolled down my eyes. 'Give me some time. I'll set everything right.'

Shagun rang up the security. In the next five minutes, a guard arrived. She took out two five hundred rupees notes and gave to the guard. 'Could you please help me with the luggage?' she said to him.

'Sure, ma'am, I'll get some more people,' he said looking at the three oversize trolley bags.

In another five minutes, he returned with three more people and rolled the bags out. Shagun took out three more notes from her handbag and gave to the guard. 'For the helpers,' she said to the guard. The guard nodded and walked out with a smile.

'You know what, Dravya?' She turned to me.

'It doesn't matter how and where we met. How it all started. What really counts is, how we got apart? How you left me for your thirst for power and money.'

'And this wound,' she touched the band-aid. 'This is what I'm taking from you as my memory. Whenever I'll look into a mirror, this wound will remind me that we are no longer together. This will tell me how we drifted apart,' her voice broke and her eyes welled up with tears.

'With time, the wound will heal but I'll keep the scar forever with me. It will always remind me that we are no longer together, that we can never be together now. Thank you for giving me this as a memory. You're not the guy who I fell in love with. You're someone else. You're a rogue. I hate you more than I ever loved you,' she said and her tears fell.

I crashed on the ground in agony and clenched my fists, struggling for control. She hates me, she hates me… That's all I could think.

You're not the guy who I fell in love with. You're someone else. You're a rogue. I hate you more than I ever loved you.

Her voice reverberated in my mind. I was shattered and broken. My towering pride crumbled. I was hit by a storm. I was quivering in pain, splintered like I didn't exist. It was unbearable.

Shagun walked away from my life, taking with her every vibrant colour of my life. I loved her enough to let her go forever.

Coffee First

'So she went?' Tanya blinked her eyes and her tears rolled down her cheeks.

'Yes,' I wiped my eyes.

'You let her go?' She grew her eyes. 'I mean, you didn't follow her? Not even till the airport or her car?'

'No,' I nodded.

'Why?' she asked softly.

'I had hurt her very deeply. I still couldn't forget her tears which she shed because of me. She was determined to begin her life again and I did not want to come in the middle. But, I carried hope in my heart. Deep down, I knew that we will reconcile.'

'You never tried to reach her?' she asked again.

'No,' I replied.

'And she? She never contacted you?'

'Never!'

'You guys won the election?' Aashi said.

'Just the election, nothing else,' I said.

'And Khushi? What about her?'

'Time made her fall in love with me. She wanted us to get married before her Master's.'

'And you? You didn't fall in love?' Tanya asked.

'I fell in love once, just once... the rest were always compromises for me,' I said.

Even after Shagun left me, I didn't call off the wedding. We won the election, but I lost my life. Simmi was right. I had made the biggest mistake of my life. No matter how much I thought I could reverse things and set them right, I could never do that.

Khushi and I were going to get married in coming June and I was still not sure whether I was going to get married or not?

'And what about Mukesh Tripathi? What happened to him?' Tanya asked.

'Shagun left me, I was traumatized. Do you think I could make any decision?' I said. 'He's alive,' I added. All of us remained quiet.

'So what happened after that? How and where did you meet Shagun?' Aashi asked to break the silence.

'You want to know?' I raised my eyebrow.

'Yes, of course, sir,' she replied.

'I want a cup of coffee first,' I smiled.

'You still want coffee?' Tanya wiped her tears and smiled.

'Yes! Why, what's wrong in having coffee?'

'You prepare coffee for him,' she turned to Aashi.

'No, I'm concentrating on the story. I'm not going anywhere,' Aashi said to Tanya, resting her elbow on her thighs, her chin on her palm. 'Come on, sir!' she said.

'I'm not telling anything. I want my coffee first.' I chuckled.

'Tanya will work on your coffee, sir. You please carry on,' Aashi said.

'No, coffee first.' I smiled.

'Tanya,' Aashi turned to her. 'Make it quick,' she said.

'We don't have time guys. If you want to know how and where I met Shagun after that, make a hot coffee for me.'

'Make it quick,' Aashi said to Tanya.

'Fine,' Tanya finally stood up to make coffee for me.

Trump Card Missing

After Shagun left, my life was completely devastated. Her absence was excruciating. I always believed that winning the elections was a key to eternal happiness. But I was mistaken. It didn't happen. Shagun was an indispensible part of my life. The night sky was sombre and starless without her.

My cards were not in my favour and do you know why? My trump card was missing. It was gone!

I was slipping into depression. Negative emotions like anger and anxiety were driving me crazy. I was nurturing a monster within me who didn't care about the worth of life any longer. I forgot to smile, I forgot what the joys of carefree laughter looked like.

They say time heals everything. Not everything…

Days turned into weeks, weeks into months and months into years. But time didn't heal my wound. It turned worse. Fury in me kept rising. I was torpid every second of my life, every single second…

Even though I was filthy rich, I was not happy. My dad became the Home Minister of Uttar Pradesh, but I was not happy. I'd lost my life. And all of this happened because my trump card was missing.

March 2020

Sid and Simmi were finally getting married. They decided to host a lavish wedding at Kerala. I was eager to attend it as something good was happening in my life after a long time.

As I entered the wedding hall, I was spellbound. Shagun was standing there in a beautiful turquoise lehenga.

My life blossomed and I smiled after three years. My eyes froze on her. I could feel my heartbeat. She had not changed even a bit, except her skin shone even more.

I was still lost gazing at her beauty when Simmi saw me and screamed, 'Dravya...' Her excited voice startled me and she left her mehendi and ran towards me. We hugged each other.

'You didn't tell me about Shagun,' I whispered.

'I invited her but I was not sure whether she was coming or not,' she said softly.

'Hmm...' We left each other.

'See,' Simmi showed me her mehendi.

'Beautiful.' I smiled.

'It's incomplete, I'll show you after an hour,' she said and grinned, showing all her teeth.

'When did Shagun come?' I asked.

'Today morning,' Simmi replied.

'But I thought you wouldn't be coming. Both my best friends are in my destination wedding, I'm super excited now.' Simmi closed her eyes and stretched the word super.

'Thanks for coming,' she added.

'Please don't be formal.' I smiled. 'I had to come.' 'Where is Sid?'

'Groom Villa is on the other side,' Simmi pointed towards the other side.

'Hey, where is Khushi? You didn't bring her?' Simmi's tone changed and she asked me quickly.

'You know, wedding season. Their entire family is in Jaipur right now. Some business friend's daughter is getting married tomorrow,' I said.

'Even you guys are getting married in June?' Simmi smiled.

'Yes,' I nodded.

'Simmi,' the mehendi girl called her. 'I've lots of hands to do,' she added.

'I'm coming,' Simmi said loudly.

'Got to go, see you around,' she turned to me.

'Of course.' I smiled. 'I'll go and meet Sid.'

'Yeah, have fun!' Simmi said and turned around to walk away.

'Simmi?' I called her.

'Yes,' she turned back.

'Should I talk to her?' I said looking at Shagun.

'Dravya...' Simmi gave me a serious look.

'She was not coming because of you. I begged her. She came today and I don't want her to go anywhere before my marriage. As it is, she's flying back to London day after tomorrow. Please don't ruin my wedding by doing anything nonsensical.'

'Hmm,' I nodded.

'Thank you for understanding,' Simmi said and walked off.

I was walking to the groom villa when I heard someone calling me, 'Dravya…' I turned back. It was Shagun.

'Hey!' I left the bag which fell on the ground.

'Hey!' she smiled feebly.

My eyes were glued to her beautiful face. I wanted to hold her nose and pull her close to me. And like always, I wanted to kiss her forehead. But it wasn't possible.

Shagun moved her hand for a formal handshake and I moved close to her, opening my arms to hug her. I then moved my hand for a handshake and she moved to hug me, opening her arms.

Both of us collapsed into gales of laughter together and that was the only thing which hadn't changed, I guess. Both of us had tears in our eyes while laughing. I wiped my eyes and she wiped hers.

'Namaste,' she joined her palms.

'Namaste.' I joined mine.

'Corona effect.' She laughed.

'Yes.' I smiled.

'How are you?' she asked.

'I'm good. What about you?'

'Happily settled in London,' she replied. 'Where is Khushi?' she asked next.

'You know her?' My voice shook.

'Simmi is still my best friend,' she replied.

'Of course.' I smiled. 'Khushi is in Jaipur. Her friend is also getting married tomorrow.'

'Okay…' She smiled. 'Specs suit you.'

My eyes rolled up to the scar on Shagun's forehead and reminded me that unfortunate episode when Shagun had left me and flew to London. Every second of that moment revolved in front of my eyes. The wound got refreshed and my heart seared once again. I was in pain, deep pain, but I couldn't share my feelings with Shagun. I was filled with remorse and shame.

'Should I go now?' Shagun asked me.

She reminded me of days when we went on dates and I dropped her back near the park. She always used to ask me before leaving. So much had changed from that moment. The girl who used to ask me before going home left everyone behind and flew to London alone. She didn't bother to inform or ask me. I got to know from Simmi.

'I should go now,' she said. Shagun turned around and walked away.

'So you finally came,' Sid screamed in happiness after our eyes met.

'You should be thankful to me.' I hugged him.

'You guys didn't come to my engagement. Why should I attend this marriage?'

'Dravya? Really? You want to start all over again?' Sid turned serious.

'Forget it!' I twigged. 'I just came.'

'Good!'

'So you're finally getting married to Simmi, huh?'

'What can I say, I'm fortunate to have her in my life forever,' he smiled and said in his excited tone.

'Yes, you're fortunate enough.' I clenched my jaws.

'Dravya,' he turned to me. He was trying his sherwaani.

'Yes,' I looked to him.

'I am sorry. I didn't mean to offend you.'

'It's okay, I understand.'

'Dravya,' he came and sat beside me. 'Shagun is here,' he said softly.

'I know. I met her.'

'You met her? Where?'

'I met Simmi before coming to you. Shagun was with her.'

'Did you guys talk?'

'Yes,' I replied.

'All okay with you guys?' he asked inquisitively.

'Yes, yes, everything is fine,' I replied. 'Forget about all this, stand up and show me how the groom looks in his sherwaani,' I said and tried to cheer up the dingy environment.

Sid stood up and adjusted his sherwaani to show me. 'How is it?' He asked after he was done.

'Handsome.' I winked.

After Shagun left, our lives radically changed. I lived in Varanasi and they were happy with their job in Gurugram. They didn't even come to my engagement. For them, I was wrong.

'You didn't tell me Shagun was coming here,' I said.

'Simmi invited her, but I didn't know she was coming,' Sid said.

'Shagun never confirmed,' he added.

'How's she?' I asked softly.

'You met her, right?'

'I met her but... You know things are not that way.'

'I understand,' Sid said and sat beside me.

'I was smitten by her. How could I do that with Shagun? I shouldn't have done that.' I buried my face in my palm.

'Dravya,' Sid kept his hand on my shoulder. 'You okay?'

'I was wrong, Sid. What I did then was wrong. I regret every second of my life. I was so lost in the game of power that I didn't even realize I was losing all of you. I didn't listen to you guys. I lost Shagun, you, Simmi, everyone. What do I have today?' I shut my eyes and let the tears roll down.

'You didn't lose us, Dravya. But yes, Shagun can never be yours now,' Sid said. 'We are always together. We're friends.'

'And Shagun?' I looked up at Sid. 'What about her?'

'Is she seeing someone in London?' I asked.

'Who knows?' Sid lifted his shoulder.

'She can't do that,' I mumbled.

'You can get engaged to Khushi, she can't even have a boyfriend?' Sid raised a question.

'Hmm…' I nodded pondering.

'Dravya,' Sid said and turned my chin to his side.

'It's over! It's been three years. You are engaged to Khushi and now you are going to get married in June. No more ruining relationships, no more messing up with lives. We all have had enough, right? As far as I know, today Khushi is irrevocably in love with you. She's very happy with this relationship. Don't make her another Shagun, please,' Sid said, looking into my eyes.

'Hmm…' I nodded.

I Deserved This

When you're broken from inside, you will go to any lengths to heal and rekindle your dampen spirits.

After seeing Shagun after three years, my love for her came onto the forefront once again. Even though Sid had asked me to move on, I still wanted to follow my heart. Shagun was sitting alone near the other side of the pool when our eyes met and I walked towards her.

'Do you mind if I join you?' I asked.

'Please, don't be formal,' she gestured me to sit.

I sat beside her, but I didn't know how to start a conversation. None of us were talking. Our eyes met and we smiled.

The evening was ornate with colourful sparkling lights. People were teeming around the bar counter at the poolside. Soothing light music and gentle breeze near the poolside caressed my heart.

Shagun's long hair flew gently, which reminded me of the days when were together. I gazed at her pink lehanga; she looked ravishing. The gold ornaments on her forehead, ears and neck made her face gleam even more.

Her light make-up embellished her face. Her matching bangles clinked whenever she moved her hand even slightly. I was dazzled by her beauty. It was tranquil. I felt like closing my eyes and hear her bangles clinking throughout my life.

'Excuse me, sir?' A waiter came to us with a bottle of scotch and glasses in a tray. 'Shall I make you a drink?'

'No,' I replied.

'Ma'am, for you?' he asked Shagun.

'No, thank you,' she smiled.

'Any kind of drink?' he asked again.

'Soft drink,' she replied and coughed.

'Sir, for you?' He then asked to me.

'Coconut water will work. Do you have some?'

'Yes sir, Kerala is famous for coconut water,' he replied smiling.

'Forget soft drink. Please get coconut water for me too,' Shagun said quickly.

'Sure,' the waiter nodded and walked away.

'So you have left boozing?' Shagun turned to me.

'Yes,' I replied. 'Why?'

'I just thought...'

'I can't break every promise,' I interrupted her and said. 'I guess I broke only one.'

Shagun didn't say a word after that.

'So how's London?' I asked.

'Beautiful,' she replied. 'Fun,' she added and sneezed.

'You don't miss India?' I asked.

'I miss my family, my friends,' she replied.

'And...?' I pulled the word.

'And what?' Her voice choked.

'You don't miss Ganga aarti of Varanasi?' Shagun tittered.

'What?' My voice rose.

'Nothing,' she replied.

'Sir, your coconut water,' the waiter arrived.

'Thank you.' I took one.

'Thank you,' Shagun said and took another.

'Both our best friends are getting married today,' I said.

'Yes,' Shagun said and sipped her drink. She coughed again.

'Are you okay?' I asked.

'Yes,' she replied.

'Just mild fever. But, I am completely alright. Hectic schedule, job pressure, travelled all the way from London, couldn't have a good sleep, attending functions here. I hope you're getting what I'm trying to say.'

'You didn't sleep well last night?' I asked.

'I was jaded. I wanted to sleep, but you know when girls get together, they have lots to talk about. And the two old college friends I'm sharing the room with, they can never stop,' she replied.

'And what about Simmi?'

'Simmi? She's busy with her cousins and family,' Shagun said coughing.

'You okay?' I asked softly.

'Yes,' she said and sipped her drink.

'I'm flying back tomorrow morning. I'll have a good sleep in London and then I'll be okay.'

'Hmm...'

'Not going to Varanasi? To meet your family?' I asked.

'They came to see me last month. It's a private job; I can't take any more leaves,' she said.

'Okay,' I said softly.

'So this June even you're getting married?' Shagun said after a moment and turned to me.

'Yes,' I replied after a second.

'You must be very happy?' she said.

'Yes!' My tears were on the verge. We remained quiet for a few minutes.

'Boo,' I said to break the silence.

'Please, I'm not your Boo,' she said breaking word to word. 'Don't call me by that name.'

'Why?' I asked softly.

'Why?' She said loudly and turned to me. 'You're asking me why, Dravya?'

I didn't turn to her; I couldn't.

'Don't you still realize what you have done? You got what you wanted and now don't expect anything from me,' she said after a few seconds. 'And don't ask me why? You know well,' she added.

She kept her coconut water and started coughing continuously.

'Boo,' I turned to her. 'Are you really okay?'

'Don't touch me,' she said and removed my hand when I tried to soothe her back.

'I told you not to call me by that name,' she said softly.

'But you're unwell,' I said.

'I'm okay,' she turned softer. 'You don't have to worry about me. I'm okay.'

Shagun stood to walk away but stumbled in her first step and sat back on the chair. She pressed her temple.

'You okay.'

'I'm feeling giddy. Get me some sugar,' she muttered.

'What?' I moved closer.

'Sugar,' she whispered.

'Sugar?' I was confused.

'Yes! Anything sweet,' she added softly. She couldn't speak.

I sprinted to the coffee counter and brought some sugar for her. 'Here,' I said, trying to catch my breath.

Shagun tore three sugar sachets back to back and diluted them in her mouth. She got normal after a few minutes.

'Are you okay now?' I asked.

'Yes,' she nodded and started swigging her coconut water.

'What happened to you?' I was still confused.

'Hypoglycemia,' she said.

'What?' I was startled. 'What is that?' I asked.

'Low blood sugar,' she said.

'What?' I reacted. I was shocked. 'Since when?'

'Since the day you broke my heart,' she replied after a few seconds.

'You were in India then?' My voice shook.

'Yes, I was working with Amazon in Delhi,' she replied.

'There was nothing to tell you. You had made up your mind that you were getting engaged to Khushi,' she said. 'Who were you for me then that I should have shared this with you? And why should I share with you? Did you ever care?' her voice shivered. 'You only cared about winning the election. Have you thought what I went through? How difficult it was for me to shift to London, have you ever thought? Have you ever thought how badly you rattled my life?' She turned to me and spluttered.

'Won the election, got seat, happy? Did you think about us?' She howled in pain.

'Ever?' She coughed.

'And by the way, thank you. Thank you for leaving me. I'm much happier now,' she said and stood up. Her snide remark intensified my pain.

'I'm feeling lousy and I have a flight to catch in the morning. I will take leave now,' she said and walked away.

I didn't say a word. I was entirely at fault. I realized everything, but it was too late. I had to let her go once again...

I wiped my tears and walked to the bar counter.

'Make me the hardest drink that you can make,' I said.

'One more,' I said as soon as he kept my first peg in front of me.

My broken heart overpowered my mind as I slipped into an abyss filled with remorse. As I drank more and more, everything seemed to fade away. I forgot everything and slept.

'Dravya,' Sid shook me.

'Yes,' I whispered and opened my eyes slowly.

'Wake up, bro. It's afternoon.'

'Afternoon?' I pulled my hair. 'Your marriage rituals? Everything done?' I asked, softly squeezing my eyes.

'Yes, I'm married now,' he said.

'Where is Simmi?'

'She's resting in her bedroom,' Sid replied.

'And Shagun?'

'She left,' he replied.

'Left?' I was startled.

'She had her flight in the morning, so she left,' Sid confirmed.

'What?' My eyes opened at once and my mouth remained half-opened. I woke up in anxiety. I had to talk,' I said softly.

'She left, now get up,' he said and stood up.

'We're having lunch together. Come on!'

Shagun left without meeting me. She didn't even come to bid adieu. She didn't even care to show me her face before leaving. Once again, I was hurt and sorrow was on its brink. Is this what I deserve? Were we strangers to each other?

After hurting Shagun, this is what I deserved.

I deserved this!

I fell back on the bed and tears rolled down my eyes.

The Turning Point

'Did you get the news?' Sid walked straight into my office and asked.

'Wait, I'm working,' I said. I didn't even look at him. I was absorbed in reading the documents of the highway extension project.

'Dravya,' he said.

'Wait, Sid. I'm working on something important,' I said. 'Give me ten minutes.'

'This is more important,' he said.

I looked at him and said, 'More important than this project?'

'Yes!'

'What is it?' I slammed the file and took off my glasses, forming curve lines on my forehead. 'Tell me, what's so important?'

'Simmi called you?' he asked.

'No,' I kept my specs on the table.

'Three people who attended my wedding function are Covid positive,' Sid said and sat in front of me.

'What?' My face lost all colour.

'Yes! And you know the most terrifying part?'

'What?' I raised my eyebrow slightly.

'The two girls who were sharing the room with Shagun are also Covid positive.'

'What?' I trembled in fear.

'Shagun is probably Covid positive,' he said. I was shocked, agonized. I lifted the glass of water and sipped twice. 'What are you saying, Sid?' I mumbled.

'How was Shagun when you met her last?' he asked.

'She was fine...' My fingers moved in the air, flinching. 'No!' I said at once and my eyes dilated with horror. I recalled something all of a sudden, something very important.

'She was unwell,' I said. 'On your marriage eve, she was coughing, sneezing and had mild fever. She was unwell, Sid,' I gasped in fear.

'And then what?'

'We were talking near the poolside. She said she wasn't feeling well and she left.'

'And the next day?' Sid asked.

'I didn't meet her,' I said.

'You didn't meet her? She went just like that?' Sid sounded surprised. 'You guys didn't meet after that, really?'

'You woke me up in the afternoon, remember?' I said.

'Yes,' Sid kept his palm on his lips.

'She didn't meet you guys?'

'No, we were in the middle of rituals when she just waved bye from far and left. The two girls who shared the room with Shagun were the first to be diagnosed,' he said and started pondering.

'Did you guys try speaking to Shagun?' I asked.

'Yes, her cell phone is switched off,' Sid replied.

'Any other number, her office or something?'

'No, we only had one number,' he replied.

'What are you saying, Sid?' I said softly. I still couldn't believe my ears. 'Did these people attend any other parties or event together?'

'No Dravya!'

'Then it's her,' I said.

'How can we be sure?' He asked.

'It's her, Sid. It's her, I know. She was really not well that day,' I said.

No matter how broken you are, no matter whether the person whom you love is with you or not, once you come to know that the person you love the most is in pain, you're ready to do anything to protect them.

Even though I was completely bewildered, I knew what I had to do next. Even though our relationship ended, I had to meet her and apologize for what I had done in the past. I had to say that even after three years of break-up, I was still in love with her.

'I'm flying to London,' I said.

'Flying to London?' Sid sounded stumped.

'Wait, what are you up to?' He moved forward.

I have to meet her,' I said.

'For what? It's over between you guys,' he said.

'It's not,' I said.

'No, Dravya, you can't do this. We're not sure, it's a guess.' He tried to comfort me.

'I'm sure,' I said in confidence. 'I can't lose her.'

'You have already lost her, Dravya,' Sid said softly. 'You can never bring her back in your life.'

'I'm flying to London, that's it!' I stood up to walk out.

'And what about Khushi? She's deeply in love with you.'

'I don't care,' I said. 'I don't care about anything. I have to meet Shagun.'

'Dravya, don't be impatient,' he said angrily.

'Impatient?' My face frowned. 'She's suffering from hypoglycemia and now she's Covid positive. Do you understand what that means?'

'I can't lose her, Sid,' I said after a pause. I was on the verge of crying.

'But we are not sure yet,' Sid said.

'I am and I don't give a damn about what you guys think.' I knew what I had to do. No one could stop me.

'Dravya, don't do this to Khushi. She does not deserve this,' he pleaded.

'And what about Shagun, Sid? Should I just leave her? She needs me, Sid. She needs me in this dire situation,' I shivered in panic. It was a horrible news. My phone rang.

'Yes?' I received the call. It was my dad.

I was unsettled with the first news, still trying to come out of the shock when another arrived on phone through my dad. I was in a fix. I trembled and fell back on my seat.

'What happened?' Sid asked.

I was not in a situation to answer anyone.

'Dravya,' Sid's voice echoed in my ears.

Once again, everything was falling apart. It seemed as if my life was invaded by a negative power which was keeping me away from Shagun. I was disturbed and shaken.

'Dravya?' Sid got up and shook me.

'The nation is going under complete lockdown from 23 March,' I mumbled.

'What?' Sid asked softly. He couldn't catch my words.

'India is going under complete lockdown from 23 March onwards,' I turned to him and said.

'What?' He was shocked.

'I'm still flying. No one can stop me.' I said.

'What? Have you lost your mind?' His face became pale.

'I don't give a damn about anything, Sid. I'm not stepping back this time. And please, don't tell anyone about the lockdown. It's highly confidential,' I said.

'Not even Simmi?' he whispered.

'Are you mad or what? No one, Sid,' I said in a strict voice. 'It's highly confidential, don't you understand?'

'Fine,' he sounded low.

Sid took a deep breath and asked, 'How will you return?'

'That's not important. Meeting Shagun is my first priority. I want to see if she is well.'

'Uncle won't let you fly,' Sid commented.

'Who's letting him know?' I added.

Sid wanted to come along with me. I knew he cared for me. He loved me as a brother. He was always there to support me. No matter how irresponsible I had been, he was always beside me. I couldn't do this. He was married now. He had his own responsibilities now. 'What about Simmi, if something goes wrong there?' I asked.

'And what about you?' he interrupted.

'Nothing will happen to me,' I said quickly.

'You know what?' Sid said after a gap. 'There's one thing that is common between you and Shagun.'

'What?' I sneered.

'You both are very stubborn,' he slid the phone to me and said. 'And it's very hard to understand you both.'

'Thank you for understanding.' I smiled.

I called up Malik and started planning how I would fly to London. Malik was unaware about the upcoming lockdown. He did what I told him to. He asked me when I would return. Now who would explain to him what I was doing and why it had to be a one-way ticket, not a round trip?

I requested him to keep this between us until I flew off to London. While the government was working on how they would deal with the outbreak, I was planning to fly abroad for Shagun.

No matter how people perceived my actions, there was no going back now. What I did in the past was wrong. It was my mistake which I didn't want to repeat. I had to meet her and convey my love.

I was not ready to give up easily this time. I was not ready to let things fall apart.

When you realize your mistakes, you can evade them. But when you get a chance to prove your love and correct yourself, you do what needs to be done. No matter how crazy it sounds.

If I could go back in time, I would like to go back to the time where it all started and rectify my actions. But you have no control over your past. You can only influence your present which affects your future. This was my opportunity to redeem myself.

Even though Sid left my office, he kept calling me, trying to convince me not to fly. He was trying hard, but even he knew that I was not going to listen to him.

I flew to Delhi and met Khushi before catching the flight. I had to tell her everything that happened in my past. I knew it wasn't worth it, but I apologized for my actions. I could feel how broken she must have felt, but this was going to be the last mistake of my life. She tried explaining to me in the restaurant, but by the end of the meeting, even she realized that I was not ready to listen to anybody.

Just like Sid, even she gave up! She dropped me at the airport.

Love has been craziest in every generation.

A Love so Pure

'This is my story,' I wiped my eyes. 'Now you know what I'm doing in this flight.'

'You love her so much,' Tanya commented. Her eyes were filled with tears.

'You wrecked everything for power and money. But, what did you gain, Dravya? I don't find anything good that has happened in your life.'

'I know.' I looked down.

'But you realized your mistake,' Aashi's voice shook while saying.

'Yes, but I was late,' I said.

'I just hope she's okay. I'll pray to god for both of you,' Tanya's voice staggered.

'Thank you.' I smiled.

'But I must say, she was very supportive,' Aashi said.

'Yes, she was,' I put on my specs.

'And she'll have to forgive you,' Tanya said.

'I just hope so,' I scoffed.

'And if she doesn't, then marry me. I'll be the luckiest girl in the world.' Aashi laughed and wiped her tears.

'What?' I guffawed.

'Yes, I am serious,' she said louder.

'What will a girl need more if she has a guy like you in her life? I'll be thankful to god for having you,' she blushed.

'I don't know how to respond to that,' I said. I looked at Tanya. She was giggling and enjoying my conversation with Aashi. 'You don't want to say anything on this?'

'No,' she kept giggling.

'Fine!'

'Can I ask you something personal? You can ignore if you don't want to answer.' Tanya asked me after Aashi was done joking with me.

'Go ahead,' I said.

'When Shagun came to Varanasi to stop you, you mentioned about her unzipping her jacket. Did you guys... I mean never...?'

'What do you think?' I winked.

'You guys must have. I mean, it's common in every relationship.' She wondered.

'And what if I say no?' I said.

'You guys never made love? I mean, really?' Tanya sounded surprised.

'No.' I smiled.

'This is the purest form of relationship,' Aashi commented. 'Which we don't see these days,' she added.

'Yes, people pretend to fall in love for all this,' Tanya said. 'And just look at you!'

'I ruined my love story. Don't pray for a guy like me. You all deserve better,' my voice quivered.

'Dravya, we're about to land,' Tanya said looking at the display when it blinked something.

'Fine,' I said looking at the display which was hard for me to understand.

'I hope you meet Shagun soon and she's alright,' Tanya turned to me and said crossing her fingers.

'I just hope so,' I said trying to build confidence in me.

'Don't worry, she'll be alright, sir,' Aashi said to boost me.

'Hmm…' I nodded, trying to control my tears which were on their way.

We exchanged our cell phone numbers. Of course, they both wanted to know whether Shagun was Covid positive or not. They also wanted me to share my photos with Shagun after I met her.

They were sure that everything would be fine. Shagun would forgive me when she'd see me coming to London for her even in this pandemic. She would forget everything and accept me in her life and we would be together forever.

The flight landed. The first thing I did was to switch on my phone. Simmi was going to send me Shagun's address.

Shagun Mehra
5 Albert Road
London
N22 7AA

Shagun's address flashed on my cell phone screen.

'Thank you,' I replied to Simmi and locked my cell phone.

I remained seated and let every passenger walk out first. I put my mask properly and stood to leave. I was the last one who walked out.

'So, when do we meet next?' I asked Tanya at the exit door.

'Whenever you say,' her smile hid behind her mask.

'When are you guys leaving?' I asked.

'In a couple of hours,' she replied.

'So let's catch up in Delhi,' I said.

'Yes, of course! I'm desperate to meet Shagun.'

'Bye,' I looked at both of them.

'Bye,' Tanya said.

'Bye, sir,' Aashi pulled her mask down and said, smiling.

I walked down the flight. I was finally in London.

The Paintings

London was frosty. I zipped my leather jacket, rubbed my palms together and exhaled warm air on them. Back in India, March was sweltering but London was pleasantly cold.

'Here, please,' I showed the address to a taxi driver.

He nodded, took my bag and kept inside. We sat in the car and the driver hit the ignition. He fastened the seatbelt and shifted the gear to take me to Shagun.

'How long will it take?' I asked.

'Almost seventeen miles from here, sir. Let us just say around forty-five minutes,' he said in his British accent. 'Which country are you from? Bangladesh?' He guessed.

'India,' I replied.

'Oh! Indiaaa...' His voice turned excited.

I couldn't see whether he was smiling or not. Almost everyone in London was in a mask.

'Colourful country,' he appreciated.

'Thank you!' I smiled.

I looked out through the window. The city was pristine and quiet. No cars honking, no commotion across the streets. The roads were well-structured and the city had towering buildings and sky-scrapers which almost touched the sky. Every street and every lane was meticulously constructed. People on the street were mostly dressed in black and I could barely see anyone without mask. The entire world was in terror.

I took a deep breath and pressed the door bell. My heartbeat raced and there were flutters in my stomach. I was so desperate to see Shagun and hold her in my arms. Every vein turned active and my eyes shimmered as Shagun could open the door anytime. I could feel my heart pounding. I pulled my mask down in excitement.

I could hear a few birds chirping. It seemed that their melodious song was for us. The cold wind swung the leaves which rustled near my feet.

There was no response. I hit the bell for the second time.

'Hold on a sec,' a voice came from the other side. Little desi type.

My face gleamed with joy and a smile awoke quickly after I heard someone coming towards the door. Probably it was the wooden flooring. My ecstasy was on its zenith which collapsed after the door opened and it was someone else. My smile disappeared in a single second.

'Shagun? Shagun Mehra? Is this her place?' I craved for her. I quickly took out my cell phone to confirm the address. I opened the address which Simmi sent me and showed to the girl.

'I'm at the correct place, right?' I confirmed.

The girl didn't look down to the address which I was showing her. Instead, she took off her mask and her eyes were glued on me. There was something wrong in the way she was staring at me. 'Is this her place?' I looked up to her.

Her lips moved a bit. She was probably trying to say something. I skipped to gallery and looked for Shagun's photo which I showed to the girl. 'I'm looking for this girl. Shagun Mehra,' I said. 'I believe this is her residence.'

'I really don't believe you're here, Dravya,' she said.

'You know me?' I was startled.

'Yes,' she said.

'How? Shagun?' I maffled.

'Come in,' she said and walked inside. I followed her.

'Please make yourself comfortable,' she said to me and gestured towards the couch. I kept my bag on the wooden floor and sat on the couch. The girl sat in front of me.

'Where is Shagun?' I asked.

'She always used to talk about you.'

'Used?' I lost my charm. 'Where is she?'

'Don't tell me the fear which brought me here is right?' I felt tremor in my life.

The girl closed her lips, trying to control her emotions, but her eyes told me what they had to. Her tears rolled down. I closed my eyes and tears fell. I soaked my throat. It was hard to believe that the fear that had brought me to London had come true. I didn't want to open my eyes. I didn't want to face the world. I felt my life was ravaged in that moment.

Shagun was Covid positive. This poignant news was the biggest disaster of my life. Her face flashed in front of my closed eyes.

She seemed even more beautiful, even more full of life. She was smiling, looking at me. The dark sky in the background was clear and the countless stars made Shagun's face shine brighter. She quickly covered her face with her palm shyly when she noticed that I was staring at her for long. She peeped through the gap which she made between her fingers. She then slowly slanted her hand down and tried to focus on me. She winked and beamed with pleasure.

'Do you want to know how I recognized you?' I heard the girl saying. I still didn't want to open my eyes.

'Dravya?' she said after a moment.

Shagun was Covid positive; I couldn't bear the pain. My heart seared. A volcano was erupting within me, which could explode anytime. How terrible the feeling was, how hard the time was, only I knew. I wish everything that was happening was an ominous dream. I wished it would vanish after I opened my eyes.

'Dravya?' I heard her again.

'Yes,' I opened my eyes.

'Do you want to know?' she asked again.

'Shagun must have showed my photos to you,' I quivered.

'Come with me,' she said and stood up.

'Where?' My voice faltered.

'I want to show you something,' she said and ascended the stairs. I followed her.

'Where are we going?' I asked. She didn't reply.

Inwardly, I was blaming myself for everything that was happening with Shagun. I shouldn't have let her go anywhere. It was my fault.

The girl opened the door for me and said, 'I think you'll need some time alone.'

'Why?' My heartbeat accelerated.

'Go in,' she said softly.

'What's in there?' I asked in agitate.

'I don't know what your reaction will be, Dravya, but you'll need some time alone.'

'What's your name?'

'Naina, Naina Modi,' she replied.

'You're scaring me, Naina,' my voice stammered.

'Just go in, Dravya. I'll wait downstairs,' she said in a reassuring voice.

Naina stopped downstairs and I entered Shagun's bedroom. My eyes shrank with tears and I struggled to regain my composure. I slumped on her bed and yelled at myself. I shouted again and again and kept punching myself. I had never hated myself this much. I was in so much pain that I couldn't resist hurting myself. Every second of my life was getting harder.

Shagun's bedroom took me to a time when we were together.

'Boo…' she whispered.

'Hmm…'

'Are you awake?'

'Hmm...' We were in our flat in Delhi.

'Do you know how I want our bedroom to be in future?'

I didn't reply. I was half-asleep.

'Boo...' She kept her hand on my head and moved my hair gently. 'Don't sleep nah, I want to talk.'

'Go ahead, I'm listening,' I responded in my sleepy voice.

'Do you want to know how I want to paint my bedroom?'

'No, I mean yes,' I said without opening my eyes.

'In the front wall, I want to paint Dashashwamedh Ghat. You know, Ganga aarti, *diyas*, and just the two of us taking part in the aarti. You remember the day when we went to the ghat for the first time? I want to have, somewhat like that. On the wall on my side, I want your smiling face. You know that special smile which you have when I'm in front of you. You may not realize it, but I do. I know the bliss of your smile, only I can feel that...On the wall to your side, I want to paint you kissing me on my forehead. The way you hold my nose and pull me close to you, I'm shy and I close my eyes. And then you kiss my forehead...

'I want to capture that feeling on the wall. And the secret behind me blushing will be between the two of us. And on the wall opposite to Dashashwamedh Ghat, the wall behind our bed, I want to paint you sitting quietly. You know, trying to make me sleep in your lap. When you'll be late from office, I'll try to sleep imagining my head in your lap.'

'I want this to happen, Boo. Will you get them painted for me?' she asked again.

'Boo..?'

'Boo...?' she said again.

'You're sleeping? I thought you were listening to me.'

'Boo,' she shook me.

'Yes, yes...' I lifted my head a bit and then fell back free.

'Boo,' she came close and whispered in my ears.

I turned to her side, opened my arms and nestled in her magical body. Her aroma worked like anaesthesia.

'Were you listening?' she asked.

'Hmm...'

'You heard me?'

'Hmm...'

'Then tell me what I said?' she asked.

'I love you,' I mumbled after a few seconds.

'Dravya,' I heard someone calling me.

'Yes,' I slowly opened my eyes. My vision was not clear. It was Naina.

'You okay?' she asked me.

'Yes,' I got up.

She had come with two cups of coffee. 'I know you love coffee,' she said.

'And what else do you know?' I asked.

'Everything, everything about you and Shagun,' she replied.

'Who are you? I mean, do you live here?' I took a cup in my hand and asked.

Naina sat on a white wooden chair placed near the window.

'Shagun and I share this apartment,' she replied.

'You too work with Amazon?' I asked.

'Yes,' she sipped her coffee.

'And what about the walls?' I looked around. I kept the coffee mug on the bedside table.

'You like them?' She asked.

'What do you think?' I responded.

'You must have loved them,' she said. 'Shagun said that she wanted a room like this with you. And one day she got this room ready. It was November, 2018,' she added.

'She settled well here?' I asked.

'No, Dravya. She was here, but her heart was always in India, with you... She was never happy here. She never made any friends here. She never tried to get anything for herself.'

My eyes were filled with tears listening to Naina. I had never thought from Shagun's perspective. She was in more pain than I was. I never cared for her. I never thought how much I was hurting her every day.

'And you know something? She said you'll be coming and you came,' Naina said.

'Before the ambulance arrived to take her, she said, "If my Boo comes to know all this, he'll leave everything behind and come to me." And you came...'

I took a deep breath and asked, 'When was she diagnosed?'

'Few days after she came back from the marriage,' Naina replied thinking.

'So today is the twelfth day,' I said.

'Any information about her? How she is?' I asked anxiously.

'Not yet,' Naina replied.

'Where is she? Which hospital, anything...?' I was growing restless.

'Northwick Park Hospital,' she replied. 'You wanna go there?'

'Yes,' I replied.

'But they won't let you in. Their Covid patient department is completely sealed. They won't allow any outsiders in,' Naina said.

'You tried?'

'No, I've quarantined myself after Shagun was diagnosed. Every part of this house was sanitized after they took Shagun.'

'You had your check-up?'I asked.

'Yes, it was negative,' Naina replied. 'They won't let you in, Dravya,' she said after a pause.

A few office colleagues went to see her last week. They didn't allow anyone to enter. They just said Shagun is struggling.'

'I have to meet her,' my voice broke.

'I can only find a way after I reach Northwick Park hospital,' I said and stood to leave. 'How far is the hospital?'

'About twenty miles,' Naina gave a guess and stood up. ' The tube will take you,' she added.

'No, I'll use taxi. Coronavirus, you know...' I said.

'Yes, taxi will be better.' We walked outside.

'Thank you for everything, Naina,' I said to her at the door.

'Take care, Dravya,' she added. We exchanged numbers.

My eyes were wet but I had a smile for Naina, which hid under my mask. Even Naina must have had a smile which was hiding behind her mask. Naina shut her door and I got into a taxi to meet my love.

Cell D23

'How may I help you, sir?' A British lady came from the other side of the counter. I couldn't see the lady's face properly. Her face was completely covered.

'I'm here to see Shagun Mehra,' my voice shrank.

'Just hold on,' she said and received her call. 'Northwick hospital enquiry, how may I help you? Hmm... Yes, yes.'

'No, ma'am, I cannot provide any information on that.'

'Yes!... Ok, thank you,' she said and hung up the phone. 'Yes sir?' She looked up at me.

'Shagun Mehra, Covid patient,' I said.

'I'm sorry, sir. I cannot provide any information on that,' she answered.

'Just tell me if she is okay?' I requested.

'I don't know, sir. I don't even know whether Miss Mehra is with us or not. You should talk on the next desk,' she said, riffling through a file.

I hopped to the next queue on the desk. People moved around desk to desk, looking for their dear ones. That havoc in the environment, unsettled atmosphere, and every panicking face around me made me fret more for Shagun. Every face that I looked at was looking for information. They all were worried.

Who could have guessed that we would be facing this day in our lives?

'Shagun, Shagun Mehra,' I said on the desk. 'I'm here to meet her.'

'I'm sorry, sir, but you cannot meet any Covid patient,' a middle-aged man said in his sharp tone. 'Next,' he shouted.

'Is she okay? I want to see her. I have come all the way from India,' I said politely.

'No information on Covid patients,' he blared again.

'Just tell me if she's okay or not? Where are the wards? Where do you keep Covid patients?' My voice shook.

'What's the patient's name?'

'Shagun Mehra,' my eyes sparked with a ray of hope.

The man started working on his desktop. 'She's still here with us. That's all the information I have,' he said looking in his desktop. 'Miss Shagun Mehra,' he mumbled.

'Where can I have more information?' I asked anxiously.

'No one here can give you any information on Covid patients,' he said.

'Doctor? Can I talk to any doctor?' I begged.

'No doctor, no patient information, nothing related to Covid.'

'The only information you can give me is Shagun is still admitted in this hospital?' I said to confirm.

The man took a deep breath and said, 'Yes!' in an irritated manner.

'Thank you,' I adjusted my mask and walked away.

I kept dashing around for almost an hour, looking for more information on Shagun when I felt my phone vibrating. I checked. It was Naina's call. 'Yes, Naina,' I received her call.

'You reached?' I heard her voice.

'Yes!'

'Any update?'

'Shagun is still here,' I said and strode looking around.

'You met her?' Her voice rose.

'No information from enquiry desk,' I replied. 'They are not letting anyone meet any Covid patient.'

'I told you. They are not even letting anyone talk to the doctors. What will doctors say, Dravya? They are trying.' She responded.

'Hmm…' I kept looking around.

'So what next?' she asked.

'I'm trying to figure out where they are keeping Covid patients. And then, I'll break in,' I replied.

'What do you mean you'll break in? This is not India,' she asserted.

'Then what should I do? Wait here?'

'You have to wait,' she said with a pause.

'I haven't come here to wait, Naina,' I said. 'Hold on, I think I found something.'

'What is it?' She asked.

'I'll call you later,' I whispered.

'Wait, what happened?'

'I think I've found where they are keeping Covid patients,' I said softly, looking at the board.

'You're going in?' Naina sounded nonplussed.

'Yes,' I said and disconnected the call.

I looked around. There was no one near the door. I slid in without thinking much.

'Sir?' I heard someone. I turned right and saw a desk. Someone was sitting, wearing a PPE kit.

'What are you doing here?' she asked.

'I'm here to meet someone,' I replied.

'Someone?' She stood up.

'My friend, my friend Shagun is admitted here. I have come all the way from India to see her,' my agitated voice broke.

'You're not allowed here, sir,' she said.

'You can talk more on the enquiry desk,' she added.

'They are not giving any information,' I blurted out. 'I need to see her, please,' I requested.

'No, sir, nobody is allowed here,' she said and walked towards me.

'It's lethal and a red zone area. Please go out,' she said pointing towards the door.

'Just let me see her once,' I pleaded.

'No, I can't let you in.' She refused.

'Please,' I requested joining hands with tears in my eyes. 'You have no idea what I have been through to reach till here.'

'I'll have to inform the security,' she said in her soft tone. 'I don't want to do this.'

'Just once,' I requested in a low tone.

'No,' she refused.

I didn't let my parents know that I was flying to London. I didn't listen to my friends who were stopping me. I broke my engagement with my fiancée and caught the last international flight taking off to London. All this was done just to meet a girl. For the girl who was just round the corner. And here, this lady was trying to stop me.

She had no idea what I had been through just to reach here. I had staked my life to reach here. She was thinking that she could stop me, but she was wrong. I had to meet Shagun.

'I'm sorry but I can't stop,' I said and headed towards the second door where the patients were isolated.

'Sir, stop!' She tried to stop me. 'Security, security,' she called for help.

I was in no mood to listen to anyone. I slammed into the ward and was astonished with what I saw. They had converted the ward into cells which had single patients in each. I was blanked out for a second. It was a sombre atmosphere.

'Sir, you can't enter like this,' a nurse stood in front of me in a PPE kit.

'Just a second, I'll be back in a jiffy,' I said and walked around looking for Shagun.

'Shagun Mehra, where is she?' I asked the nurse and started searching every cell.

'I need to see her,' I said in a bold voice.

'What are you doing, sir? You're disturbing everyone here,' another face arrived in front of me. "Every face around me was wearing a PPE kit."

'I'm here for Shagun Mehra, where is she?' I asked quickly and continued searching the cells.

'You should leave this place. It's not safe for you.' I heard one of them saying.

'I don't care,' I said and searched for Shagun. 'I don't want to disturb anyone here. Just tell me where is Shagun. I need to see her.'

I was motivated. I had no idea where I got this power and energy from all of a sudden.

Every cell I entered, I was expecting Shagun to be in there. My eyes were desperate to see her. My hands were ready to hold her and with every step, every cell, my heart was gesturing me that I was getting closer to Shagun. There was some sort of change in the environment which I felt whenever I used to be close to Shagun.

People were stopping me, but I was ignoring them. I only knew one thing, I was very close to Shagun and I had to meet her. Four people were trying hard to stop me, but I had made up my mind. I was not going out without meeting her.

No matter what would be the consequences, I will meet her.

'You'll get infected this way, sir,' I heard a voice.

'I don't care! What will happen? I'll die? Anyway I'm dying without her. I'm dying every second of my life.'

'And once again I'm telling you guys, I'm not here to disturb anyone. Just tell me where is Shagun Mehra? Tell me her cell number.'

'You think Covid 19 pandemic is a trivial matter?'

'No, not at all, but meeting Shagun is my first priority,' I said loudly.

'Hey, you, stop!' Someone came in front of me. 'Who are you? What are you doing here?'

'Doctor, we are stopping him, but he's not listening to us,' one of them said.

'What are you doing in here? Is this a joke to you?' the doctor asked.

'I'm looking for my friend,' I replied softly.

'This is not a joke. Get out of here!' he said.

'I'm not going anywhere without meeting my friend. And I'm not taking anything as a joke here. I know what's happening. My country is going under lockdown from Monday onwards. Even then, I caught the last flight just to meet my friend who is admitted in this hospital.

'I don't know how long I'll be stuck here. I don't know when I'll reach my country. Whether I'll reach or not. But I don't care about anything.

'I've to meet Shagun,' I felt my voice collapsing.

'Shagun? That Indian girl?' The doctor pointed his thumb backward and said.

'Yes!' My face brightened. His words brought colour in my life.

I felt relief after seeing his thumb pointing backward. I got excited. I had goose bumps all over my body. I was about to meet her; I finally found her. I was so excited to meet Shagun that when I plunged the doctor aside in excitement and ran to her, I didn't even realize.

I hastened a few hands and then started checking the cells randomly. Doctors, nurses, staff members, they all froze. I behaved so madly that no one tried to stop me after I pushed the doctor aside. Every part of me was desperate.

As I ran to find Shagun's cell, my mind went back to some beautiful moments of the past, probably our last romantic moments.

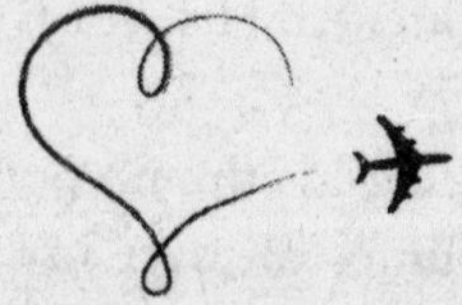

The Flashback of Love

'I love you,' I said.

I was in Varanasi and Shagun was in Delhi. I was helping my dad in elections.

'Hmm...' she responded.

'When will you say "I love you" in front of me? You are able to express yourself on messages, but never on a video call,' I asked.

'Does it matter?' she asked softly.

'What do you think?' I added.

'I think what really matters should be how much we love each other. How we feel for each other.'

'I cannot capture my feelings in words,' she added. 'Do you know how much I love you?'

'No,' I giggled.

'No?' Her tone changed.

'You tell me how much you love me,' I insisted.

'Place your palm on your heart and close your eyes,' she said softly.

'Why?' I asked.

'Just do it, Boo,' she said.

'Okay, done,' I said and closed my eyes after placing my palm on my heart.

'Do you hear my name?' she asked after a pause.

'Yes,' I said softly.

'What do you feel?' she asked after another pause.

'I feel you,' I said, smiling.

'Now do you know how much I love you?'

'Yes,' I replied.

'This is what happens to me when I place my palm on my heart. I hear your name.'

'When you're busy somewhere and I miss you, I want to talk to you… I do this. I close my eyes and hear your name. And when I do this, I feel a smile on my face. The lovely smile that appears when I think of you. I feel you around me…'

'I might not be able to describe well, but I love you. I may run short of words but my affection for you grows every day. And I hope you understand…'

'And even if you don't, I won't be upset. I'll try to explain you. You're my life, Boo,' her voice shook.

'You're crying?' I asked.

'No,' she replied.

'Then your voice…?'

'Can I ask something?' she interrupted.

'Yes, yes.'

'You won't leave me nah?' she asked softly.

'No, Boo, why are you saying this?' I was surprised.

'No, I mean, circumstances might bring a lot of hurdles in our lives...'

'It will never happen,' I said quickly. 'No one can separate us.'

'You trust me?' I asked with a pause when she didn't say a word.

'Hmm... More than anyone in this world,' I responded.

'The day you leave me, Boo, I will die. I might breathe, but my soul will be gone...'

'Why are you saying all this?' I interrupted her.

'Because I want you to know how much I love you. I want you to know what will happen to me if you leave me.'

'I'm not leaving you,' I said.

'And what if time separates us?' she asked.

'Then I'll run after you. I won't let you go anywhere,' I said. 'No matter where you'll be, no matter how challenging the situation, I will follow you till my last breath.'

'I look in the mirror and think how I can always keep you happy. What I can do for you that will keep you always close to me.'

'You're sitting in front of a mirror right now?' I asked.

'Yes!'

I left my bed and switched on the lights. I stood in front of the mirror. Shagun was right. Even my face was blazing with tears. I was listening very carefully to her every word and tears were rolling down. Her words were filled with pure emotions. Every drop of tear had something to say. I could feel them...

'Boo, you're crying?' Her tone changed.

'No,' I replied. I was trying hard not to let her know.

'Yes, you are! I'm making a video call.'

'No,' I said wiping my tears.

'You're taking my call. Come on Skype,' she said and disconnected the call.

'What?' I received her call.

'Come close and show me your eyes,' she said.

'See,' I moved close.

'Yes, you were. You were even sounding glum on phone,' she said.

'No.' I smiled.

'Yes, you were, Boo,' her eyes were filled with tears.

'No,' I said again and kept my smile. My tears stood on the verge. I was trying not to let them fall.

'I'm sorry, they're because of me,' she said and her tears broke free.

I closed my eyes after seeing her tears. I couldn't stop mine anymore.

We both remained quiet and let our eyes talk. In the hushed night, starts fell on our love and the two souls remained together, thinking the night would never end.

'I love you,' I said softly.

Her face tingled and she looked down. Her hair fell over her face and I could see her lips smiling. 'Hmm...' She nodded.

An Irreparable Loss

'Where is she?' I came back to the doctor.

'You pointed in that direction. I didn't find her,' I said pointing in the same direction as the doctor.

'I'm sorry,' he said.

'What? Where is she?'

'You saw her,' he said.

'I saw her?' My face turned pale.

'Cell D23,' he said.

I turned around and rushed towards D23. I stopped outside D23. I took a deep breath and tried to calm myself. I was panting. I tried to catch my heavy breath and entered the cell.

The entire world collapsed. Thunder and lightning stroke my heart and I felt my soul sinking gradually. I was broken and devastated.

Tears froze on the edge. I wanted to believe what I was seeing was untrue. Probably, I had entered the wrong cell. My feet shivered in anxiety. I wanted to step out of the cell, but my heart didn't allow. I couldn't make out what was happening. In just a single second, everything fell apart. With every breath, every part of my body was turning numb.

A body was wrapped in a white cloth. It was completely sealed from top to bottom.

'We couldn't save her,' I heard someone behind me. 'We are sorry for your loss.'

'I think I'm in the wrong cell,' my voice quivered. 'This can't be her.'

'It's hard to believe, but you have to stay strong,' the voice continued.

'Is she really my Shagun?' I turned back.

'Yes,' the doctor nodded.

'It can't be, it can't be...'

'Stay strong,' he said.

'She's not my Shagun,' I said. 'I'm looking for someone else.'

'She was a brave girl. Though she was a hypoglycaemia patient, she was fighting against Covid 19, but...'

My breath was caught in my throat. 'We're sorry for your loss,' he said.

'She was struggling since morning. She couldn't even breathe properly. Our ICU was occupied, so we were shifting her to another hospital. But it was too late by then. Our ambulance was not free, and by the time another ambulance reached here, it was late...

'There was a word which she kept repeating during her last breath. Boo... I think she was calling someone. Like, she wanted to see someone for the last time. She knew her death was near, but she was expecting someone.'

'Get her file,' the doctor said to one of the staff members.

'Here,' he then handed over the file to me. 'We had only one Indian Covid patient.'

I opened the file and saw Shagun's report.

'She left us an hour ago. We were processing the formalities to shift the body,' he said.

The file slipped off my hand and I lugged myself at Shagun. I tried to untie her.

'Stop him,' the doctor said to others.

They all caught my hands and didn't let me see her.

'You can't do this, sir,' one of them said. 'She was a Covid patient. You should stay strong and walk out. You might get infected.'

'I... I need to see her face....' My voice shook.

'You can't,' he said softly. 'We can understand your pain.'

'If you understand my pain, then let me do this,' I said softly.

'Sorry, we can't let you,' he said.

'I don't care if I get infected. I don't care even if I die, but please, please let me see her for the last time.'

"The man turned to the doctor. The doctor nodded and left."

They pulled me out of the cell. They didn't let me see her. Not even for the last time...

I could no longer fight back. I had no strength left. I was faltering. Shagun was dead and I was going to end my life soon. My tears... They didn't fall. They remained frozen. It was my fault. Shagun died because of me. I killed her. I wanted to cry, but no tears came. I wanted them to fall, but they had given up on me. Shagun took my tears with her. And this was adding more pain to my life.

I was left outside the Covid ward. There was another tumult felt by people around me. The Prime Minister of UK had just announced a complete lockdown. But, I didn't really care about anything anymore.

Naina called me up, and then Sid, and a minute later, Simmi. I didn't receive any of their calls. As UK was also going under lockdown, they all were jittery and dazed.

All I knew was, I couldn't fulfil Shagun's last wish, the doctor didn't let me see her and I deserved this. I lost my Shagun forever.

Epilogue
2022

I was sleeping when my phone buzzed. It was Sid. I received his call, 'Yes, Sid.'

'I've landed safely,' he said.

'Dravya?' I heard his voice when I was about to disconnect the call.

'Hmm...' I replied.

'I still don't understand why you're doing this,' he said.

'It's been two years, why don't you get over and move on? You can't spend your entire life in Shagun's bedroom,' he added.

'You came here to explain the same. Could you?' I asked.

'No,' he said after a pause.

'Then why now?' I asked.

'Because I care for you. We all care for you. And what you're doing is incomprehensible,' he said.

'You'll never understand, Sid.'

'Dravya...' He was about to speak when I interrupted.

'Sid, please! You all can never get me back there. I'm fine here. Please leave me alone.'

'You have nothing in London. Please come back, come back for your family, for us...' he requested.

'I have everything in London,' I said. 'Shagun is around me. I feel her...'

'Dravya...'

'I was sleeping, Sid. Can I? Please?'

'Hmm, take care,' he said.

'You too, bye,' I said and disconnected the call.

I was still asleep when the maid came to my room and drew the curtains. The gloomy room illuminated as the sunrays fell on the wall. I opened my eyes.

'On the wall to your side, I want to paint you kissing me on my forehead. The way you hold my nose and pull me close to you. I feel shy and I close my eyes. And then, you kiss my forehead... I want to capture that feeling on the wall.'

'And the secret behind my blushing will be known to just the two of us.'

'And Boo, one more thing,' she said. 'We have to take care of the direction of the windows. You want to know why?'

'Early in the morning, when we will draw the curtains, the golden sun rays will fall directly on the wall and its glow will lighten up our faces. Our love will blossom, and grow forever in our eyes...'

Her words echoed in my ears, every morning after the maid drew the curtains aside. That's how my day began. I kept thinking about Shagun's words and closed my eyes.

I could feel tears in my eyes, but it never fell. I tried but I failed every day. Shagun was still not ready to return my tears to me…

'Boo, you don't want to return my tears? Fine! But there were things I wanted to say after meeting you. Shall I?'

The day I broke your heart and you left, I wanted to…